W9-BVM-657

DAUGHTERS OF THE MOON

the choice

Also in the
DAUGHTERS OF THE MOON
series:

DAUGHTERS OF THE MOON

the choice

LYNNE EWING

HYPERION/NEW YORK

First Edition
1 3 5 7 9 10 8 6 4 2
Printed in the United States of America

Library of Congress Cataloging-in-Publication Data
Ewing, Lynne.
The choice / Lynne Ewing.
p.   cm. — (Daughters of the moon; 9)
Summary: Amid premonitions of her own death, Jimena travels to the past and teams
up with her old gang rival, Payasa, to try to save herself and the other goddesses from
the evil Atrox and its Followers.
ISBN 0-7868-0851-9
[1. Supernatural—Fiction. 2. Time travel—Fiction. 3. Los Angeles (Calif.)—Fiction.]
I. Title.
PZ7.E965 Ch 2003
[Fic]—dc21
2002033939

Visit www.volobooks.com

For Julie Christine Morales

—————ᴗᴗᴗ—————

▼

In ancient times, the Gorgon Medusa lived on the far side of Oceanus in the land of Night. She was an awesome dragonlike creature with bronze claws, great golden wings, and fierce eyes that turned her beholder to stone. At one time she had been a beautiful young woman who filled the world with joy, not death, but in a moment of foolish pride she had compared herself to Athena. Such arrogance enraged the noble goddess, and in revenge she turned Medusa's lush hair into a tangle of vile, hissing snakes. From that moment on, Medusa's stare brought the stillness of death to anyone who dared look into her eyes.

Meanwhile Polydectes, King of Seriphos, wanted to destroy Perseus, so he sent him off to bring back Medusa's head, knowing that her gaze would kill the young hero. But Athena heard the king's command. Still angry with Medusa, she gave Perseus her bronze shield to defend himself when he attacked the Gorgon. Holding the shield as a mirror, Perseus saw only Medusa's reflection, and her deadly stare did not harm him. He cut off her head and put it into a cloth bag, then flew away with the aid of a pair of winged sandals given to him by Hermes.

As Perseus soared over the African desert, blood seeped through the bag and fell to the hot sands below. As each drop hit the scorching ground, it turned to steam, and the rising vapors transformed into three dangerously beautiful nymphs.

CHAPTER ONE

JIMENA CASTILLO HIT the street hard. The impact slammed through her, leaving her stunned and unable to breathe. She pressed her cheek against the hot asphalt and closed her mind to the memory of her friends calling for her as they were swept into a hellish black cloud. She wanted to scream out her sorrow, but no sound came from her empty lungs.

Only minutes before her life had seemed dream perfect. She liked her new friends at La Brea High, and she had finally found a boyfriend who didn't care about her past. She pictured Collin. Maybe she was even in love with him.

All of that was lost to her now unless she could find a way to change the future.

Jimena tried to convince herself that coming back to the past had been the right choice. She had believed it was the only way to save Tianna, Vanessa, and Serena, but the guilty cramp in her stomach told her she should have stayed and faced death with them.

The growing rumble of a truck motor made her blink and glance up. A brown UPS truck sped toward her, the driver searching for addresses, not watching the road ahead. Maybe she was going to face death, after all. The tight pain in her chest held her paralyzed. She lay stone still, waiting.

The truck horn blared. Gears shifted down, metal grinding. The front wheels locked, and the truck kept coming. At the last moment, it swerved, the tires inches from her face, spitting grit and grime into her open mouth. The stench of burning rubber filled her nostrils.

"You stupid druggie!" the driver yelled from

the open truck door, more fear in his eyes than anger. "If you're going to destroy yourself, you don't have to take the rest of us with you."

Suddenly, her lungs worked again. She gasped, sucking in exhaust fumes, then coughed and wheezed. Hot pain jolted through her. Slowly her body remembered the soft rhythm of breathing. She pushed up to her knees, shaking her head against the dizziness, then grabbed the truck door frame and pulled herself up.

"Sorry," she whispered at the driver.

He shook his head with scorn.

"What's the date?" she asked. She didn't even know the year in which she had landed. How far back had she traveled?

"Get out of the street before you cause an accident." The driver jerked the truck into gear and it rolled away.

She limped to the curb, stepped onto the sidewalk, and brushed dirt from her skirt, arms, and legs. She breathed the spicy smells of frying onions and chilies from the taco stand on the corner and tried to figure out where she was.

In the distance the familiar shining office buildings of the Los Angeles skyline stood tall in the smoggy brown air. Behind her, faded stuffed animals pressed against the barred glass of a liquor store, their black eyes peering over advertisements for cigarettes, *cerveza*, and lottery tickets. Next door a fanfare of lace and satin filled the window, waves of *quinceañera* dresses jamming the display.

She didn't need to see more. She was on the wrong side of Wilshire Boulevard, east of Alvarado. Enemy territory. That was dangerous, but it could have been worse. At least she had landed in Los Angeles. Now she only needed to find out how far back in time she had traveled. She looked up and down the street for a newspaper stand. When she didn't see one, she decided to head toward MacArthur Park before any of her old *enemigos* caught her on their land.

She had only taken one step when a shadow darted into her peripheral vision. Her heartbeat quickened, and a thin haunted cry escaped her lips. She turned, terrified that the deadly cloud from the future had somehow followed her into the past.

But it was only her old rival Payasa standing behind her.

"*¿De dónde?*" Payasa sauntered toward her, head thrown back, joy on her face. She wore a blue plaid Pendleton jacket over khakis. Harsh, thick liner circled her defiant eyes.

Her real name was Graciela. Payasa was her *placa*. It meant "clown." Her street name came from the way she wore her makeup, definitely not from her sense of humor. She brushed back her thick bleached hair and stopped, her face inches from Jimena's. "I said, where you—"

"I know what you said," Jimena interrupted, and pushed away from her. "I don't have time for your stupid war games."

Payasa grabbed Jimena's shoulder and yanked her back.

"You're in my neighborhood now," Payasa warned.

Old anger awakened in Jimena. She tensed, trying to push it back. She was still down for

Ninth Street, her old gang, but at age fifteen she had quit the life when she had discovered her true destiny. She lifted Payasa's hand from her shoulder, her stare issuing a warning of her own. "*¿Nueve, y qué?*" she said. "What are you going to do about it?"

Payasa flashed a hard smile. Her lips were outlined in the same black eyebrow pencil she used to draw arches over her dark eyes. She had shaved her eyebrows, and the lines replacing them curved onto her forehead. "Why are you here, bitch?"

"I fell from the sky." Jimena couldn't resist teasing her old foe. Her answer was also true. If anyone had seen her arrive, it would have looked as if she had abruptly materialized in midair and plunged to the street below, barely missing the oncoming traffic.

"You think I'm not serious?" Payasa blinked as if she enjoyed the sweep of her false lashes on her cheeks.

"*Claro*, you're serious." Jimena matched Payasa's threatening posture, leaning her head back, jutting her chin out. "That only proves you know nothing about the real *peligro* in Los Angeles. If you knew the true danger, you wouldn't be wasting your time fighting over broken-down neighborhoods that don't even belong to you."

Jimena wondered what Payasa would do if she did tell her the truth. Would she even believe her?

"I'm *your* danger." Payasa inched back the shirttail of her Pendleton, revealing the black handgun tucked into the waistband of her jeans. The butt rested against the *Payasa* tattooed across her tight, flat stomach in Old English lettering.

"I'm not scared of you." Jimena folded her arms across her chest with confidence. A holstered gun couldn't shoot anyone but the owner.

"You should be." Payasa bared her teeth in a wicked grin. "I got the power."

"I never needed a gun to make people afraid of me." Jimena smirked. "You don't even have half my reputation."

"*Vamos a ver,*" Payasa answered, with too much boldness.

Then Jimena saw the reason for her

arrogance. Three girls from Payasa's *klika* pushed through the screen door of the liquor store. Jimena had gone to school with them before she had transferred to La Brea High.

Mimi and Pilar strutted outside, sucking on Tootsie Pops, the white sticks bobbing in their mouths. Mimi could still wear the jeans she had worn in seventh grade, but Pilar filled the doorway. She had gone out for defensive tackle on the high-school football team and was proud of the way she had made the guys eat grass. She wore the team jersey.

Lara followed after them, wearing a bulky blue jacket, too heavy for the day. Jimena knew they had been shoplifting inside and hidden their loot in pockets sewn to the jacket's inside lining. Bottles clanked each time Lara moved.

"Look what I found." Payasa motioned with her head. "Risky from *El Nueve*."

Risky was Jimena's gang name. It was tattooed over her hipbone.

The three homegirls circled her, faces blank. Even though they were used to not letting their emotion show, Jimena could tell they were scared.

She smiled, satisfied. They were afraid of her, even at four against one. Her reputation was still legend. In the old days when she was banging hard, she had fought them and won, but she didn't have time today. Besides, she wasn't dressed for it. Her arms and belly were bare, her earrings too long and easily yanked from an earlobe. Even her spike-heeled sandals were the wrong ones for a mix. Only moments before, she had been at a rock concert in the Staples Center. She slowed her breathing, suddenly aware Lara was also checking out her clothes.

"So how come you're in our neighborhood dressed for a party?" Lara asked in a fiery tone.

Jimena pushed around Lara. "I don't have time for wanna-bes."

Pilar and Mimi eased together, blocking her way.

Payasa joined them, a thin cold smile crossing her face. The tip of her red dagger nail tapped the butt of her gun. "Don't be in such a hurry. We got all the time in the world."

"I don't." Jimena grabbed Mimi's shoulders and wheeled her aside.

Lara stepped in front of her. "Now, you do." She slipped from her heavy coat and let it fall behind her. The bottles clanked together.

"We just want to party with you." Payasa's hand slipped around the gun in her waistband. Her index finger curled into the trigger.

Jimena understood the threat. They were going to jump her, and if she ran, Payasa was going to shoot her.

"It'll take more than the four of you to drop me," Jimena said, answering their challenge.

Anger fired across Payasa's face. "You still think you're the toughest *chola* in *el condado*. We're going to make you nothing." Her hand left the gun. She scooped her long hair into a ponytail and tied it with the scrunchie on her wrist, getting ready to fight.

"If you knew the facts," Jimena said, "you wouldn't be messing with me."

"What facts?" Payasa asked, suddenly alert.

Jimena didn't need to be a mind reader to

know Payasa was worried Jimena might have set them up. She had their attention now. She considered what to do next. Did she dare tell them the truth? There was no reason to keep her identity a secret now. If she couldn't find a way to change the future and stop the Atrox from kidnapping her friends, the world as they knew it would cease to exist. She shook her head. They wouldn't believe her even if she did tell them she was a goddess, a Daughter of the Moon, and that she was here to protect people from the primal source of evil. They'd just think it was some *tecato* fantasy.

Pilar tapped the end of her pop on Jimena's chin. "*Oye*, Payasa wants to know what facts."

Jimena slapped the pop away, suddenly overcome with the need to return to the future and help her friends. The red candy shattered on the sidewalk. "I don't have time for this. What day is it?"

"What kind of *yesca* have you been smoking?" Payasa asked. "You think we're not going to jump you if you act stupid?"

"Just tell me," Jimena ordered, her frustration rising.

The circle closed around her. Lara, Pilar, and Mimi glanced at Payasa, waiting for her order.

Then without warning, Jimena's vision began to blur.

"No," she whispered, blinking rapidly. Sudden fear dropped over her. She couldn't do this now. Since she was a little girl she had had premonitions about the future. She had never been able to stop one from coming, but falling into a trance right now in enemy land with her old nemesis Payasa ready to blast her was too dangerous.

The sharp anger left Payasa's face, replaced by an odd fear, as if she had witnessed something inexplicable and arcane in Jimena's eyes. The others stepped back with abrupt nervousness. What had they seen on her face?

Before she could consider it more, the white, glaring sunlight began to fade as if clouds had crossed the sun, then shadows swept around her in a phantom dance, pulling her into another world. She strained against the pull of the hypnotic state gripping her, but it absorbed her, and she fell inside herself.

The vision roared up to meet her, smashing through her with a force that made her head wrench back. Then everything became still and dark. Finally, a small light appeared in the distance, seeming to be at the end of a long tunnel. It grew into a ball of white fire and invited her to follow it, but she stepped back, afraid, knowing that if she went forward she would fuse with it. A chill spread over her and she began to tremble. Death was calling her.

Bitter sorrow spread through her. She didn't want to die, but her anguish wasn't for herself alone. If she died, her friends would be lost as well. Did the premonition mean she had failed?

The mental picture faded. She shook her head, trying to rid her mind of the last murky images. How long had she been standing oblivious in a trance while Payasa and the others watched? It couldn't have been more than seconds, but it felt as if she had been gone for hours.

She wiped at her tears with the palm of her right hand and caught Mimi's worried look.

"What did you see?" Mimi asked and pressed the edge of her finger against her teeth.

"*Nada*," Jimena answered slowly. "Nothing." She understood their uneasiness now. Lara and Mimi had called her *brujita*—little witch girl—in elementary school, because even at a young age Jimena had had the ability to see the future. But back then she hadn't known that she was having premonitions. She had thought she was making the bad things happen.

"You think she saw something about us?" Lara whispered.

"I hope not," Pilar said. "Remember Miranda?"

Jimena pressed her right hand against her chest, trying to ease her rapid heartbeat. The first time she had had a premonition she had only been seven years old. She had seen her best friend,

Miranda, in a white casket. Then Miranda had touched her, and another picture had flashed across her mind of Miranda walking down the street as a car sped by, a gun in the window blasting bullets. She had tried to protect Miranda, but she hadn't been able to keep death from taking her. Since then she had never been able to stop one from coming true, not even with help from the other Daughters of the Moon. Now she knew it meant she was going to die soon. She bit her lip. A joyless feeling wrapped around her, strangling her other emotions.

"Are you trying to scare us with that old trick?" Payasa spit at Jimena's foot. "That *trampa* won't work on us."

Her words gave the others courage, and the air filled with the edgy tension that always came before a fight.

"She's just faking it," Lara agreed, shifting her weight for better balance. "Maybe it used to work, *brujita*, but you can't scare us away with your witchy games anymore."

Mimi looked unsure, but when Pilar slipped

closer, so did she, her hands hungry for the first punch.

Jimena tensed, nerves raw, her head still aching from the premonition. Maybe Payasa and her *klika* were going to deliver the death she had seen.

CHAPTER TWO

PAYASA LURCHED FORWARD, her jaw clenched. Her arm hooked back and she swung. Jimena ducked, the punch skimming over her head. Payasa looked surprised.

Jimena grinned. "Next time."

Then fists were everywhere, slamming and missing by inches. In frustration, Lara started to kick. Jimena scooted to the side, grabbed Lara's ankle, and swung her off balance.

A man from the liquor store came out. "Stop it, you punks!"

His yelling gave Jimena the distraction she

needed. She jumped up and back as Payasa came at her again. She shoved Mimi aside and started to flee, but Pilar snagged her, clamping her huge hands around her waist. Jimena twisted wildly, fighting to break free, but every time she turned, Pilar's fingernails dug deeper into her bare stomach, scraping away skin.

"I said, stop it!" the man yelled. His words were brave, but he didn't try to help her.

Finally, Jimena rammed her elbow into Pilar's ribs. Pilar moaned and her grip loosened. Jimena bolted free.

"*Puro* Ninth Street! *¡Rifamos!*" she yelled, and dodged into the street without checking the oncoming traffic.

A tow truck sped past her. The mud flap hit her leg as she ran behind it. She glanced over her shoulder, hoping the others would be too afraid of the speeding cars to chase after her. Lara, Pilar, and Mimi hesitated, but Payasa shoved through them and vaulted off the curb, eyes focused on Jimena.

Jimena raced around a white Suburu and

stepped into the path of a speeding Kawasaki motorcycle. The startled rider throttled down. The front fender caught her skirt. She ripped the silky material free, then placed her hand on the headlight and kicked out of her sandals. She caught her reflection in the black visor of his helmet. Her hair had tangled. Streaks of mascara ran down her cheeks, making her eyes look fierce.

She took off again, her bare feet slapping the gritty double yellow lines in the middle of the road, arms pumping at her sides. Pebbles and bits of glass cut into her soles. She looked for a break in traffic. She needed to cross to the other side of the boulevard before Payasa caught up to her.

Cars bearing down on her flashed their headlights in warning. Horns blasted until the honking became one loud ceaseless clamor. This is what her day-to-day life had been before Maggie Craven had told her about her true destiny. Jimena thought back to that moment.

Maggie had spoken to her in Latin at their first meeting. *"Tu es dea, filia lunae."*

Jimena had been stunned that she understood the words. She couldn't know Latin. It had to be some trick of hypnosis.

Maggie had laughed and told her that she knew ancient Greek as well, then she had repeated, "You are a goddess, a Daughter of the Moon. The proof is in your ability to see the future. It is a gift from Selene, the goddess of the moon, because you will need that power to fight the Atrox and its Followers."

A car drifting over the center line jolted Jimena back to the present.

"*¡Wátchala!*" she yelled in Spanglish. She jumped out of the way as the driver steered back, too busy talking into his cell phone to notice the world around him. Jimena shook her head and took off again, her lungs on fire.

Brakes squealed behind her. She glanced back and her foot slammed into a rain-filled pothole. Her ankle twisted painfully. She paused, hopping on one foot.

An RV had almost hit Payasa. The driver opened the cab door and started to get out, his face red under a crop of prickly white beard and yellowed shaggy hair. His hands reached out as if he needed to touch Payasa to make sure he hadn't hurt her, but Payasa yanked away from him and pulled out her gun. She waved him back into the car. Payasa scanned the traffic, looking for Jimena.

Jimena ducked behind a Volvo, using it as a shield. The passenger peered downward, scrutinizing Jimena. The automatic locks snapped down.

"Go, go!" the passenger yelled, her voice wild with fear.

The Volvo lurched forward, almost hitting the Buick in front of it.

As soon as the traffic cleared, the car sped away. Jimena didn't move quickly enough, and the door handle thumped against her shoulder.

Payasa saw her.

Jimena stood and started running again, eager for a break in the traffic. She needed to find a place to hide. She was totally exposed now.

Payasa's heavy work boots struck the pavement, sounding louder with each step.

Jimena glanced back.

Payasa's gun was drawn, tight against her side, her eyes waiting for the right moment to fire, but Jimena knew the gun was too heavy for Payasa to shoot on a run. The recoil would jolt through her arm and knock her shoulder back, making her hand buck and her aim sloppy.

Payasa fired anyway. The cracking thunder drowned other sounds. Sparks flashed off the pavement where the bullet had hit. Bits of stone shot free, slicing into Jimena's leg. The bullet ricocheted and struck the side of a black sedan. Somewhere a woman screamed.

"Damn," Jimena muttered, grabbing for her leg. She hobbled into the slowing traffic.

Drivers looked frantically around, trying to find the danger. Jimena skirted around the cars and dashed across the street.

There was an alley only a few yards in front of her between two brick buildings, one an old hotel and the other a small grocery store with displays of fruit near the entrance.

In spite of the pain, she quickened her stride,

sidestepped a crate of apples, and darted into the alley.

A newspaper slapped lazily against a discarded tire. She scooped it up and kept running, turning the paper to find the date. Wednesday! She had less time than she had thought. Then another thought struck her: maybe she had even less. After all, the paper had been trashed. Could Catty have made an error that big?

In a reckless attempt to change the future, Catty had dropped Jimena somewhere in the past, hoping Jimena could find a way to change the future and stop the Atrox from capturing Vanessa, Serena, and Tianna.

Like Jimena, Catty was a Daughter of the Moon, but her gift was time travel. She could go back and forth through a hole in time she called "the tunnel." She had said she was only going to take Jimena back one week, but her time travel had never been accurate. She was still learning how to use her power. Now, Jimena wondered if Catty had only taken her back a few hours.

Distant sirens filled the air. Probably four or

five drivers had used their cell phones to call the police. She looked for a place to hide. Two Dumpsters hunkered at odd angles against the wall ahead of her. If she could get behind the last one she'd be safe for a few minutes at least.

She quickened her pace. The sweet, putrid smell of garbage filled her lungs as she ran past the first of the battered orange bins. She looked over her shoulder, straining her neck to see the front of the alley, fearful Payasa would appear, gun in hand, and shoot. She started to turn her head back and collided with someone.

Her teeth snapped painfully together. She tried to pull away and dive behind the Dumpster, but the person held her tight. She struggled against the restraining arms, then a familiar silver badge flashed in front of her eyes.

"LAPD," a commanding voice said.

Jimena understood the implied order in those words. She stopped moving.

"Jimena?" the same voice asked, softening.

The arms released her. She turned. Two Los Angeles police officers stood behind her. Officers

Perez and Bekin. They had special assignments to do gang suppression. She had known them back in her old gang days.

"Hey, hi," she said, breathless, her feet stinging from the cuts, each draw of breath sending new pain through her chest. She tried to pull her face into a smile but knew it was a strained imitation.

She glanced back at the alley entrance. Payasa strolled by, gun now concealed, her face a mask. She looked like any neighborhood kid on her way home from school.

Jimena let out a sigh.

"Are you all right, Jimena?" Officer Perez lifted her sunglasses. Her eyes fixed on Jimena, watching for a lie.

"Sure." Jimena nodded. "Things couldn't be better." But the words choked in her throat, and she caught the quick exchange of glances between the officers.

"What were you running from?" Officer Bekin asked, his back stiff, the seams of his pantlegs so crisp it looked as if he never bent his knees.

"Just, you know, jogging," Jimena answered. She wasn't a *rata*, not even for the enemy.

"You don't look like you're dressed for a jog." Officer Perez's gaze was forceful now.

Jimena glanced down at her bare, muddy feet. Her blue skirt was torn and covered with street oil. Blood trickled from the scratches on her exposed midriff and the nicks on her legs. She licked her lips, feeling restless. She didn't have time for their interrogation. "The spirit came over me. Haven't you ever just felt like, you know, running?"

"Running down the middle of Wilshire Boulevard, obstructing traffic, is that what you mean?" Officer Bekin asked.

"No," Jimena answered, agitated.

"We heard gunfire." Officer Perez motioned toward the street with a nod of her head. "Is that why you were running?"

Before she could answer, the next question was hurled at her.

"Who was chasing you?" Officer Bekin glanced behind Jimena as if he expected a gang of hoodlums to come skidding around the corner.

"No one," Jimena said. Then, unexpectedly, the haunting echoes of her friends' cries came to her, calling her back to the future, making her feel still more distressed. She needed to find out what day it was—and quickly.

"You look like someone was after you," Officer Perez concluded.

Jimena shook her head, trying to quell the panicked feeling that time was running out. "*¿Qué fecha es?*" she asked without thinking.

"*¿Mande?*" Officer Perez looked confused. She blinked rapidly, as if trying to clear her thoughts.

"The day," Jimena repeated too loudly. "What day is it?"

Officer Bekin's expression hardened. "What day do you think it is?"

Jimena paused. She didn't have the answer. "Wednesday?" It was her best guess.

"It's not Wednesday," Officer Perez corrected her, and moved closer, scrutinizing Jimena's eyes, then scanning down to the crook in her arm, and finally checking her ankles for needle marks.

Jimena was disheveled and dirty, her party dress smeared with grease, and she had been acting like a druggie, running down an alley for no apparent reason, drenched in sweat, her heart racing. She hadn't seen the officer running toward her until she had slammed into him. Then not knowing what day it was sealed it. That's all they had needed to convince them that she had been doing drugs.

She sighed. "It's not what you think."

"I'll call it in." Officer Bekin walked back to the squad car parked at the other end of the alley. His shiny black shoes crunched over shards of broken beer bottles.

Jimena knew what this meant. He was going to run a make on her. "I don't do drugs," she said.

"Are you still doing your community service, Jimena?" Officer Perez asked, her thumbs hooking into her gun belt.

"Yeah, I go over to Children's Hospital. I

love spending time with the kids." Jimena had been in Youth Authority camp twice. She would have gone back a third time for firing a gun if a lenient judge hadn't sentenced her to do community service work instead. She worked with children undergoing rehabilitation for gunshots wounds.

"You know if someone has been bothering you, it's safe to tell me." Officer Perez took on a maternal tone and her eyes seemed to soften.

"No one's been bothering me." Jimena looked away.

After a few moments, the sound of footsteps made her look back.

Officer Bekin walked toward them, his stride slow and easy.

"Can I go now?" Jimena asked.

In answer, he snapped open the leather case on his gun belt and pulled out a pair of handcuffs. "Have you been doing business at raves, Jimena?"

"No," she answered, baffled.

"Come on, Jimena," he said and stopped in

front of her. "Let's go." He motioned for her to turn around.

"Since when is running barefoot against the law?" Jimena asked, desperate to find out what they had on her.

"Put your hands behind your head," Officer Perez said, her voice sad.

"But I haven't done anything!" Jimena glanced back to the alley entrance.

Payasa had reappeared, arms folded across her chest, an insolent smile on her face.

"An ecstasy ring was busted." Officer Bekin locked the first cuff around Jimena's left wrist with a loud click. He brought her other hand down. "One of the dealers named you as the supplier."

"It's a lie," Jimena argued.

"We'll see," he answered.

"At least tell me what day it is!" she pleaded.

"Thursday," Officer Perez answered.

Jimena's heart raced with alarm. The concert was on the following Sunday night. What could she do now? Coming back to the past had been her last hope for saving the others. She squeezed her eyes against the burning tears. She wouldn't let Payasa see her cry. Besides, crying couldn't help her now. Nothing could.

CHAPTER THREE

J

IMENA SAT IN THE back of the squad car, handcuffs digging into her wrists, and breathed the lingering scent of stale coffee as uninvited memories of Sunday night came back to her.

Catty, Serena, Vanessa, and Tianna had invited her to a concert at the Staples Center. Afterward they had planned a coed sleepover at Serena's house to celebrate Jimena's sixteenth birthday. Monday was a school holiday, and they were going to spend it at the beach.

Jimena had had high expectations for the

sleepover. Collin had often told her how much he cared for her, but she had never had the nerve to reveal the depth of her feelings to him. She liked him more than a lot. Maybe it was even love. She had planned to tell him so at the sleepover, then she had hoped he would confide in her and let her know what had been bothering him lately.

Jimena had hidden her own emotions enough times to know when someone else was doing the same. She thought about that now. Even in their last telephone conversation Collin had held back. She knew there was something more he had wanted to tell her but when she had pressed him, he had said it was nothing

She pictured Collin, remembering their last kiss, and a delicious warm feeling spread through her. More than anything she wished she could wake up, cuddled in his arms, and discover that all of this was only a nightmare.

Sunday afternoon had started out ordinarily enough. She had been in San Diego, helping in her uncle's restaurant, and had missed the first Greyhound bus leaving for Los Angeles. She had arrived at the end of the concert as the band ran off the stage.

The audience had been clapping and yelling for an encore. Their screams rose higher and higher until the noise became one deafening shrill whistle.

Then Jimena became aware of an electrical thrum against her chest. When she glanced down, the silver moon amulet hanging around her neck was glowing. The charm had been given to her at birth. Serena, Catty, Vanessa, and Tianna each had one, too. The ornaments warned them when danger was near.

But that night she ignored its alarm because the band came back on stage, playing their most popular hit. Pyrotechnics exploded around the singer, and the audience went wild, dancing, waving glow sticks and singing along.

Then a slow thick thunder spread through the Staples Center. The vibrations traveled up her legs and through her spine. At first she had thought it was part of the act, but then the lead singer pulled out the plug for his in-ear monitor and tilted his head as if he were trying to uncover the source of the reverberation.

The guy on bass guitar turned and checked the plugs linked to his amplifier, looking for a faulty connection.

The rumbling grew, resounding in the walls.

Jimena looked at the giant monitor hanging from the rafters. The singer continued his song, but his eyes connected with something overhead, not the audience.

A huge unnatural shadow formed, slipping across the west side of the building and eclipsing the spotlights sweeping over the crowd.

Another concussion boomed. This time roadies ran on stage, checking lines and equipment.

A palpable change filled the air as an evil vibration pulsed through the audience. Hands that had been waving glow sticks stopped. Everyone became still, looking at the phantom silhouette looming above them, their faces filled with fear.

Suddenly, the audience surged toward the

exits, shouting and calling to each other, some screaming in terror. Jimena was pushed backward in a crush of kids. She struggled through them to a row of seats, then stepped over the backs of chairs, trying to reach her friends.

Catty, Serena, Vanessa, and Tianna stood together, their moon amulets blazing, eyes dilated as energy rose inside them. When they locked their arms to combine their powers, a gold aura shimmered around them. Before they could release their energy, the shadow whipped down and sucked Vanessa into its billowing blackness.

Jimena jostled over the remaining seats and joined them as the black form charged down and tore Serena away.

"No," Jimena yelled, grasping for Serena too late.

Serena looked down at Jimena, her eyes wide with fear, and screamed for Jimena to save her as she was swirled up and into the cloud. Her glow stick fell from her hand, and Jimena caught it.

The air shuddered with an eerie howling.

"It's coming back." Catty said, breathless

with fear. "The Atrox has never attacked us like this before. It always sends others. What's happening?"

Tianna hooked arms with Jimena and Catty. "We can defeat it."

The demon shadow struck again and tore Tianna into its vortex.

It swirled in anger, gathering above them.

"Use your power to take us away," Jimena had urged. "We can't beat it."

"But the others?" Catty had asked, her eyes fixed on the evil storm.

"Take us back. Any place." Jimena didn't understand Catty's hesitation. "It's our only chance. Do it now!"

The cold vapors of the Atrox swarmed down, surging around them.

At the last possible moment the tunnel flashed open with a brilliant white light and sucked them inside. They spiraled backward in time.

Catty had then dropped Jimena somewhere in the past, promising to return after she went into the future to see what more was going to happen. But she had never come back. Now Jimena had a sinking feeling that the Atrox had captured her as well.

Jimena needed to warn the Daughters of what awaited them at the concert this coming Sunday, but she couldn't do that now. How was she going to change the future from jail?

▼

CHAPTER FOUR

IT WAS PAST MIDNIGHT when Jimena was finally inside the juvenile detention center. She had been sent to closed custody, where she would be told when to sleep, eat, and shower. She glanced down at her plastic jail ID bracelet. It was the same kind used in hospitals to identify patients.

"What size do you wear?" a large-boned girl asked. *Lenox* was tattooed on her throat, and she smelled of tobacco and coffee.

"Seven," Jimena answered, aware of the deputy behind her breathing over her head.

"Here's your blues." The girl handed Jimena blue cotton pants with an elastic waist and a matching short-sleeved shirt. *Los Angeles County Jail* was printed in black down the left pant leg and across the top of the shirt.

Jimena took the clothes with a heavy sigh and walked down the glaring polished linoleum to the next room.

"Next door to your right," the deputy said.

They turned into what looked like a dressing room in a department store, except that none of the cubicles had a door or a modesty curtain, and a large square bench sat in the middle of each booth.

Rage surged through Jimena, and she blinked back hot, angry tears. She knew what came next, and the only way to survive it was to force herself to go numb. Indifferent. She took her place between too partitions.

The deputy stood at the opening, arms braced across her chest. "Strip down."

Jimena took off her clothes and waited, naked.

"Run your fingers through your hair," the deputy ordered.

Jimena did.

"Lift your breasts."

Jimena followed the instruction, her mind already finding another safer place.

"Turn around and . . ."

Her mind curled up tighter. The remaining orders came, and she did what she was told without thinking or feeling.

Eventually, the deputy was satisfied that Jimena had not brought any contraband with her. "Okay, put on your blues and we'll get another picture taken."

Jimena slipped into her clothes.

She was still seeing blue-gray spots from the camera flash when at last she was given her roll-up: two blankets, one sheet, one towel, and another pair of underwear and socks.

Then they went outside and walked across the tarmac. Jimena sucked in the cold air, trying to rid herself of the claustrophobic feeling that had tightened around her. Overhead floodlights lit the long rows of beige buildings. High fences with coils of barbed wire circled each structure.

"Here we are. F-one." The deputy pulled at the key holder on her gun belt.

Jimena stopped and waited. The chain links in the fence had a curious bend at eye level, as if too many inmates had gripped the mesh, longing to be outside.

The deputy unlocked the gate and pulled it back.

"Inside." She motioned with her head. "Nose to the wall."

Jimena entered the compound, squeezed the roll tight against her chest, and stood inches from the stucco facade.

The deputy looked down at a white paper as she unlocked the door to the dorm. "Castillo, you're assigned bunk twenty-five."

The door swung open, and Jimena stepped inside. The sour smell of sleeping bodies rushed over her, bringing back the tight choking feeling. The door closed, darkness swallowed her, and the dead bolt slid into the striker plate.

She waited for her eyes to adjust to the dimness inside, then stepped down the rows of bunks, listening to the slow, steady rhythm of sleeping inmates and a dripping faucet. Someone coughed. Another thrashed in her sleep.

Thirty-two cots with one-inch-thick mattresses lined either side of the room.

She found bunk twenty-five, but another girl was sleeping there, her arms and legs pulled into a prenatal curl, the sheet wrapped over her head. Jimena unrolled her blanket on the floor beside the bed and lay down.

She had been given a yellow nightgown. Now she wadded it into a ball and used it as a pillow. Tears slid down her cheeks, and she didn't stop them this time.

A restless sleep took her, and then the dream came. She was in a long, thin boat. The oarsman tried to take her across the river, but she fought the forward movement, jamming her hands into the cold water and using them as paddles, trying to keep the craft from reaching the other side.

A voice on a loudspeaker startled her awake. She jolted upright. Bare feet came down on top of her and then she remembered where she was.

"You have five minutes to line up," the voice repeated as a deputy opened the door.

Girls threw off their nightgowns and frantically changed into their blues. Others, like Jimena, who had slept in their clothes, walked outside to the fence and waited in the cold gray morning while the deputy did her count.

Inmates stared at Jimena, checking her out. Some exchanged secret smiles of recognition. Others looked away, nervously avoiding her stare, and pretended to scope out the weather. All looked older and harder than their teenage years.

"Okay, you can go back to your dorm," the deputy said after the count had been completed.

As soon as Jimena claimed her cot, the house mom approached her in slow, sure steps. She was a girl in custody who had been voted into her position by the other girls in the dorm. The blue scarf around her neck identified her rank. Blurred tattoos marked her knuckles. It looked as if she had used ink and a straight pin to write her boyfriend's name on them, and had later tried to change the letters, or blot them out. "You came in last night?"

Jimena nodded. "Someone was sleeping in my bunk. Number twenty-five."

She shrugged. "I'm Janna." She lifted Jimena's hand and read the plastic wristband.

"Jimena." Janna smiled warmly. "It's easy here if you follow the rules."

A voice on the PA interrupted. "F-one, line up for chow."

"Keep your hands in your waistband," Janna continued as they stepped toward the door. "And don't talk on the way to mess hall. No talking while we eat either. If you get caught talking, you have to throw out your food and stand at the wall."

Janna fell into the single-file line.

"I'll explain the rest later." She pressed her lips together and stepped out the door.

Jimena glanced at the parade of girls in front of her. They marched to the mess hall, silent and resentful, hands jammed into their waistbands, faces stiff.

The air outside was still and filled with the promise of a hot day. Jimena surveyed the buildings and fences, desperate to find a way to escape. She listened for traffic sounds but heard nothing. Even if she did get out, it would take the rest of the day to make it back to Los Angeles.

Inside the dining room, she picked up a scratched metal tray. Yellowish liquid ran from her scrambled eggs and seeped into three gray sausages. A carton of milk sat at an angle, leaning on a still-green banana.

They had fifteen minutes to eat. Even though she was hungry, the food felt like acid in her stomach. No one looked as if the meal had been enough to fill the emptiness inside them. Some ran their fingers around the grooves in the trays, then licked the last trace of flavor from their fingers.

After breakfast they were marched back to

the dorm. Most of the girls crawled onto their cots and tried to sleep.

A girl with long scars and bumps on her arms sat on the bed across from Jimena. "I'm your bunky." Her smile showed off her broken teeth. "They call me Smiley."

"I'm Jimena."

Smiley started unwinding her pigtails. "I got a dirty reading. You, too?"

"I don't do drugs," Jimena answered.

Smiley snorted. "Then why are you in F-one? Everyone knows they divide the girls into houses depending on their crime. F-one is for druggies like me."

Jimena shrugged. "An ecstasy ring got busted and the dealers said I was the supplier."

"You get the names of the ratheads?" Smiley asked, as if she might know them.

Jimena shook her head. Everyone knew the love drug was the number-one drug problem in L.A. Kids even sold it in the hallways at La Brea High, but Jimena never had.

She stared out the window, remembering the

Christmas when she was four. Her mother had overdosed on the couch in their small studio apartment. Jimena had called 911. The police had come and seemed disgusted with her mother. No one told her if her mother was going to be okay.

She had seen her mother only once after that, the day she walked away. Now she could no longer remember her mother's face, but she still remembered the terror of that afternoon, alone in the apartment, trying to wake her.

How could the cops think she'd get involved in trafficking? She'd never follow her mother into that graveyard of trouble.

A breeze came through the window, caressing her cheek and bringing her back to the present. Clouds glided across the sky. She thought of Collin, her friends, and her grandmother. She didn't want to leave them, but she could feel her death coming closer. If she could drift out of the world in her sleep it might not be so bad, but she had a terrible feeling that it was going to be a hard way out.

The slow rumble of a motor made her look to the east side of camp. Dust swept across the tarmac as a bus pulled in and parked.

"Newcomers!" Smiley shouted.

Other inmates rushed to the windows, jeering and yelling threats to the new arrivals. Their hands shook the mesh screens until it sounded like maracas rattling.

The first girl off the bus looked frightened and exhausted. Her chains pulled her shoulders down in defeat, but the three behind her didn't seem intimidated. Cold smiles stretched across their faces. They were dressed causally in jeans and short-cropped sweaters, their long lush hair blowing around their backs.

An evil aura emanated from them, and in spite of the heat, a chill crept up Jimena's back. The trio had to be Followers. Jimena glanced down to see if her moon amulet was glowing, but then she remembered it had been confiscated.

She glanced up again.

"What's with those three?" Smiley asked.

"What do you mean?" Jimena wondered if Smiley could feel their evil.

"Man, they are wicked weird," Smiley said. "They're acting like they're happy to be here. What kind of attitude is that?"

With a shudder, Jimena realized the truth. The trio was here to end her life. With Jimena dead, no one would be able to save the Daughters, and the Atrox could rule the world.

The guards took the three girls into a building. The door closed but their afterimages remained, hovering at the entrance.

Jimena sucked in air.

Giant shimmering wings curled from the backs of their ghostly forms. The wings seemed more reptilian than angelic, soft membranes stretched over thin, narrow bones. Slender claws extended from their fingers, like the talons of birds of prey, capable of ripping flesh. Delicate gold scales sparkled on their arms, and slippery black snakes twisted in their hair, tongues flickering.

Jimena was awestruck. She had never

seen anything look so terrifying and yet so beautiful.

The phantom figures turned and stared at her, green eyes stormy, as if they had just found what they were looking for.

CHAPTER FIVE

AFTER LUNCH, JIMENA sat on her cot and watched the three new girls. Azera stretched her hands over her thighs and licked her lips as if she had just tasted something delicious. Zonda sat on the bunk next to her, her gaze intimidating. The third one, Lizelle, had an eerie sweetness in her voice. She turned now, her green eyes fierce, and grinned at Jimena, but her smile was like the warning of an animal baring its teeth.

Jimena needed to escape before they attacked her. If her dorm hadn't been in lockdown, she was certain they would have tried already.

Someone in their dormitory had passed a kite, a letter, to one of the girls in another section. As a result the inmates in F-I had to stay seated on the edge of their cots. No one could even get up to use the rest room. The only sound came from a girl who was ripping her sheet into long strips to make rags to curl her hair.

Jimena wasn't allowed to use her powers to do things like break out of jail, but she no longer had a choice. If she didn't leave soon, it would be too late.

She studied the metal door. The force inside her had stopped Followers. That same energy had to be strong enough to blast the door off its hinges and stun the guards. But was it too deadly? She didn't want to hurt anyone.

When she had fought Followers, the strength inside her grew automatically, but she had never tried to generate it when she wasn't defending herself. She wondered if she could. She concentrated, and the room came into sharp focus. Energy raced through her with an intensity that made her tremble.

Smiley glanced at her. "What is it?" she asked in a low voice, her eyes wary.

Blue sparks crackled around Jimena as her power surged.

Smiley gasped and tried to smooth down wisps of her hair affected by the static electricity in the air.

Jimena stared at the metal door, her concentration intense. Dancing lights shot from the tips of her fingers. She started to send out a spike of energy, but the doorknob turned. Someone was coming inside.

She stopped abruptly. A tangle of silver-blue flashes pierced her skin as she drew back her charge. She winced and swallowed hard, pain exploding inside her.

A large woman stepped into the dorm, her uniform stained with sweat. A man followed her, pushing a huge red bucket on rickety casters.

"Deputies in the house!" the woman yelled. The door slammed against the wall with a loud boom.

The man shoved the bucket to the side,

wheels squealing, then pulled out a pair of heavy shackles.

The woman deputy lifted a white paper on a clipboard. "These are the people going to court. When I call your name and number, line up. Castillo five-three-three."

Jimena glanced down at the last three numbers on her bracelet to make sure they wanted her and not someone else with the same last name, then she stood and walked over to the bucket. The energy continued to dissolve inside her and made her legs feel awkward and unsure.

The deputy took the chain with attached handcuffs and locked it around Jimena's waist. The links felt cold and heavy against her flat stomach.

Lizelle's name and number were called. She sauntered over and stood beside Jimena.

The deputy locked a shackle around her slender body, then he took the cuff hanging on the left side of Lizelle's chain and snapped it around Jimena's wrist. He grabbed the cuff dangling on Jimena's right and locked it on Lizelle's wrist. They were chained together now and forced to stand close to each other.

"Perfect." Lizelle smirked as the deputy restrained their free hands in the cuffs at their sides.

He pushed the bucket to Zonda and Azera, and began shackling them together.

The first deputy finished calling out names. Twenty or more girls had been summoned to court.

"After you're shackled, head out to the bus," she yelled and fanned herself with the clipboard.

Jimena and Lizelle walked together like Siamese twins; one couldn't move without the cooperation of the other.

"I'm the one who set you up," Lizelle whispered as they crossed the dead grass to the tarmac. The chains and cuffs clanked together, beating a rhythm that sounded like a tambourine.

Jimena stared at the bus waiting for them, her mind working on a way to escape.

"Aren't you going to ask why?" Lizelle said.

Jimena ignored her. She knew the reason; the Atrox had planned it all to stop her.

An unnatural breeze puffed around Jimena. She turned her head. A dragonlike image was superimposed over Lizelle. Giant wings flapped lazily, stirring the air and creating swirls of dust devils. A crown of snakes hissed in her lush hair.

Jimena's breath caught and she blinked, trying to rid her eyes of the image.

A deputy helped Jimena onto the bus, her muscles tight and strong. Behind her sunglasses, she squinted against the debris twirling in the wind, but she didn't act as if she sensed anything unusual about the dust clouds forming around them.

The dragon creature had to be an illusion that only Jimena could see. Her heart raced as fear spread through her.

Lizelle climbed onto the step next to her; the silky wings wrapped around her as her phantom form squeezed into the bus. Fine shimmering scales coated her skin, but her face didn't look monstrous. Jimena felt spellbound by her beauty.

"Move on," the deputy ordered.

Only then did Jimena realize that she had

been staring into Lizelle's eyes, unable to pull away. She shook her head and continued carefully up the steps, then shuffled sideways to the back of the bus, her steps clumsy and tripping over the tips of Lizelle's wings.

They pressed together in their assigned seat, the handcuffs on their joined sides digging into their flesh.

A coal-black snake slithered from Lizelle's hair to Jimena's shoulder. She glanced at the inmates hobbling onto the bus. No one saw it.

The snake twisted toward her, tongue flicking. She clenched her teeth, trying to convince herself that it was only an illusion, but when it curled around her neck, its skin felt dry and soft, and she knew it was real.

A low miserable moan struggled up her throat. The deputy glanced at her, then back at the line of inmates stumbling into their seats.

"No one is going to help you," Lizelle whispered. "No one."

CHAPTER SIX

THE DEPUTY STEPPED down the aisle, holding the metal handrail for support, and did a head count, her lips moving silently. Then, satisfied, she walked back to the front of the bus and locked the wire gate separating the inmates from the cab.

"Ready," she said.

The driver shifted gears, and the bus pulled away. The air coming through the roof ventilation hatch reeked of exhaust and gasoline, then cleared when the bus passed through the front gates and headed down a two-lane road toward Los Angeles.

Zonda and Azera turned, looking over their shoulders at Jimena, their faces impossibly beautiful.

"Pretty necklace," Azera said. "Is it real snakeskin?"

That made Zonda snicker. Then they both smiled, their eyes burning with promise, as if they had planned something far worse than the snake wrapped around her neck.

"Jimena," Lizelle said, her voice dangerously sweet and hypnotic. "Look at me."

Jimena tried to summon her power to protect herself from the attack she sensed coming, but no force surged inside her. Were they doing this to her? Or had she done this to herself. Perhaps her power functioned like an electric battery, and hers had burned itself out.

"Jimena," Lizelle called again in her siren voice.

"What?" she answered angrily and glanced at Lizelle. She froze, stunned again by Lizelle's unearthly perfection. The eyes were compelling, clear and deep, rimmed with dark lashes. Jimena stared into them, fascinated.

A strange coldness flowed through her body. It wasn't the chill of a winter day, but something internal and deep. Her heart labored inside her chest as if her blood had become too thick and heavy to pass through her arteries and flow into her body. Its slowing beat pounded inside her chest.

The tips of her fingers turned icy, then numb. She tried to move her hand but couldn't.

She summoned all her strength and wrenched away from Lizelle's gaze. She gasped, her breathing difficult as if the muscles in her chest had tightened into rigid bands.

She glanced at her hand. The skin no longer looked soft and supple but hard, glossy, and dead white. With great effort, she moved her thumb against her index finger. The hardness of her flesh frightened her.

"Like stone," Lizelle whispered, as if she had read Jimena's thoughts.

Jimena started to yell for the deputies, but her jaw was locked, teeth clamped together. She could not move her tongue or lips.

Her eyelids became too heavy and slowly closed. The hum of the bus motor grew more distant and then silence surrounded her.

Her mind tried to cling to reality. But why not just give up the struggle? Her premonition had shown her that she had no future anyway. Maybe this was the darkness that her vision had foretold.

CHAPTER SEVEN

EVEN WITH HER eyes closed, Jimena sensed a change of light inside the bus. She struggled to lift her eyelids and through a veil of lashes saw a streak of sunlight coming toward her. At first she thought it was only a reflection from a passing car, but as the gold light came closer, the rigid cold inside her began to melt.

The brightness wrapped around Jimena as if forming a shield to protect her. Warmth returned to her body, and immediately a soft and pleasant tremble began growing inside her.

She had felt this same prickling sensation

when Vanessa had made her invisible. That was Vanessa's gift, but Jimena was certain the glow surrounding her now wasn't her friend, so who had come to rescue her? An angel? Another goddess?

Then a darker thought intruded. Could a Follower be stealing her away? Some Followers had the ability to dissolve into shadow and stay that way for days. But she had never heard of a shape changer becoming a dazzling light. Besides, whoever or whatever it was had to be a source of good, because she didn't feel afraid.

Suddenly, her hearing returned, and an abrupt noise made her jump. Shrill cries pierced her ears. Lizelle shrieked like a carrion bird that had lost its prey. Zonda and Azera joined her. Their dragon apparitions floated over their human forms. The giant wings beat with a frenzy, creating blustering winds inside the small bus.

Jimena was able to open her eyes all the way now.

One deputy unlocked the gate and two more stepped down the aisle, unsnapping their holsters and pulling guns. They turned in cautious circles looking for a target, the wind flapping their uniforms against their bodies.

Jimena's skin began to ripple as bone and muscle stretched.

"No!" Lizelle screamed and rattled the chain around her waist.

An inmate sitting across from Jimena gasped. "What's happening to you?" Her hair whirled about her face as if she were caught in a storm.

Jimena glanced down. Her hands, no longer stone, looked fuzzy.

"Stop her!" Azera yelled, frantic.

A deputy pitched forward, gun aimed at Jimena. Her mouth dropped open when she saw Jimena's blurring hands, arms, and legs. In reflex, her finger pulled the trigger. White flames licked the end of the gun barrel and an ear-piecing thunderclap filled the air.

The bullet blasted through Jimena's hand with stinging fire, but she was no more than a swirl of specks now. Her body spread and became a phantom, levitating into the air. The shackles slipped through her and dropped onto the bus seat.

Her hazy silhouette drifted over the deputy's head, guided by the gleaming light, and then she became completely invisible.

The bus filled with screams and the racket of clanking chains.

The light wrapped around her, then dove and pulled her through a crack in the driver's open window into the freeway traffic. A truck bore down on Jimena and the force controlling her, its silver grille inches from smashing into them and scattering Jimena's molecules. Abruptly whatever power held her soared into the sky, taking her with it, and then they were gliding with the seagulls that had come inland.

They rode the wind high above the San Gabriel Valley, up and over sprawling homes perched on the hills in Pasadena. Finally, they skimmed the tops of pine trees, and the scent of mountain air breezed through them.

When they were on the far side of the San Gabriel Mountains, they drifted lower, scraping through spiny evergreen branches to the ground.

Jimena materialized on the rim of the Angeles Crest Highway, looking down a thousand-foot drop. But as her molecules came together, her weight grew too heavy for the fragile sandstone ledge. Pebbles and sand slipped down the steep rock. Then clumps gave way beneath her feet. She swung her arms, trying to find balance, and started to tumble over the edge.

CHAPTER EIGHT

OUT OF NOWHERE, strong solid hands grabbed Jimena around the waist and pulled her back to the paved road. She turned.

"Chris?" The last time she had seen him, he had been a student at La Brea High. Back then, she had thought he was just another good-looking guy with a great smile and spiky hair. Catty had later told her that he was really the keeper of an ancient manuscript called the Secret Scroll. It described the only way to destroy the Atrox.

"I hope I didn't scare you." Chris gently

took the snake from around her neck and set it on the road. It slithered across the rock-strewn highway and slipped beneath some dried weeds.

"Thanks for rescuing me." She stared at Chris now, dumbfounded. She had never noticed before how extraordinarily blue his eyes were. "Does Catty know you're back?"

Chris shook his head.

"She'd want to know," Jimena said.

"I can't let anyone know my whereabouts."

"Catty isn't just *anyone*." Chris had fallen in love with Catty, but after the Scroll had been lost, he had left to search for it. He had promised to return to her some day.

"I won't risk putting her life in danger," he said softly.

Jimena put her hand on her hip and tilted her head. "But it's okay to risk mine?"

"You're already in mortal danger." He put a comforting arm around her and rubbed her back as if he knew what she had been through.

She nodded, disheartened.

They wandered down the empty road, their shadows stretching in front of them.

"I shouldn't have shown myself to you either," Chris said. "But I couldn't let them destroy you yet."

"Yet? You make it sound like it's my destiny to be destroyed."

A crow flew over head, and its sudden appearance seemed to unnerve him. He pulled her into the dry grass under a fir tree. Grasshoppers danced around their feet, and wind sighed through the low-hanging branches.

"You're the only one who can save Catty now." He glanced back the way they had come.

"Why can't you?" Jimena asked.

His eyes filled with sadness. "I have to find the Scroll."

She started to speak but he stopped her. She caught his look and knew he was trying to find a way to tell her something terrible. She felt heartsick. What could be worse than what she had just been through? Her stomach dropped.

He took her hands and glanced down at the

strange red welt where the bullet had passed through the stretched-out molecules of her palm. When he looked up at her again, his expression was tender. "Jimena—"

A twig snapped. He turned sharply and yanked her behind a tree trunk.

"What is it?" She looked around, rubbing her wrists where the handcuffs had cut into her skin.

"It could have been someone sent back from the future," he whispered. "They'll do anything to stop you."

"Those weird dragon girls?" she asked. "What kind of Followers are they?"

"They're not Followers," he answered.

Her heart raced. "What are they then?"

"They're nymphs," he explained. "They've been sent to destroy you before you can change the future back to the one that was meant to be."

"But aren't nymphs supposed to be fun-loving spirits who live in forests and help humans?" Jimena asked.

"Most are," Chris agreed. "But these were

formed from the blood of the Gorgon sister Medusa."

"You mean the monster who turned men to stone?" Jimena remembered how she had felt cold and paralyzed when she gazed into Lizelle's eyes.

"She wasn't a monster," Chris went on. "She had once been beautiful, but when she compared herself to Athena, the goddess changed her into something deadly. After that her gaze turned her beholders to stone, but men still risked death for one glimpse of her beauty."

"I know the story." Jimena felt stunned to think that the myth could be true. "Perseus used Athena's bronze shield so that he didn't have to look at Medusa directly."

Chris nodded. "He cut off her head, then placed it in a magic pouch and flew away. But drops of her blood fell on the desert and created three nymphs."

"Lizelle, Zonda, and Azera," Jimena whispered. She started to say more, but Chris placed two fingers on her lips, cautioning her to be silent.

He looked overhead. "Something's coming."

Sunlight flickered down through the swaying branches. Jimena felt—more than heard—a distant rumble. "Is that the nymphs?"

Chris shook his head and backed away from her. "I can't be seen. You mustn't tell anyone you saw me, not even Catty. If the Atrox discovers I'm here, it will send its Regulators."

The Atrox wanted to destroy the Scroll, and had ordered its internal police force, the Regulators, to capture the manuscript and its keeper.

Chris began to dissolve. His body undulated like a gold mist in the forest gloom.

"Wait," Jimena cried out. "How am I going to get back to L.A.?"

He continued to fade. His mouth moved, but she couldn't understand what he was trying to tell her.

"How do I change the future?" she yelled after him.

It was too late. He was no more than sunlight gliding around the tree trunks.

The rumbling suddenly became louder.

A police helicopter shot toward her. Cold fear clutched her. She knew intuitively that the people on board were searching for her, but she didn't understand how they could know she'd be in the mountains above Los Angeles. She'd only been there a few minutes.

Jimena darted into the murky shadows. She felt sure no one in the helicopter could spot her, but then she remembered the heat-sensitive technology that law enforcement used now. They would be able to see her like a ghost image on their screen.

Quickly, she grabbed a rotting tree branch and pulled it over her as she curled into a tight ball. Ants, insects, and tiny white worms dropped onto her from the decaying wood. She cradled her head beneath the log and hoped the image the officers in the helicopter received didn't look human.

The helicopter circled. The downdraft from the rotor blades bent the treetops, and a storm of dry pine needles and cones rained over her.

Finally the helicopter darted away.

When the rumbling faded, she tossed the log aside, slapped the insects and worms from her clothes and brushed them from her face and hair. Her sense of urgency was overwhelming. Even if she walked quickly she wouldn't be able to reach L.A. before early morning. She could hitchhike, but traffic was sparse, and no one was going to give a ride to someone wearing county blues. She sighed heavily and followed the highway from behind a camouflage of trees.

The darkness had taken on an eerie gloom by the time she came to a dirt road that twisted farther up the mountain. A sign read CAMP-GROUND. She hated what she was going to do next, but she had no choice. She was cold, hungry, and thirsty. She took the turn.

At the first campsite, lanterns sat on a picnic table near two tents. A huge fire was burning in a cement pit in the center of the clearing. A family of five sat gathered around the blaze, roasting hot dogs and marshmallows on long sticks. She breathed in the smells, and her stomach squeezed with hunger.

A teenage boy bundled in a coat, cap, and heavy gloves began telling a ghost story. The others seemed captivated.

Jimena slipped forward with quick stealthy steps and stole into the first tent. Sleeping bags had been neatly rolled out. A pile of clothes sat in one corner. She lifted a bulky red sweater, a knit cap, and yellow gloves, then ducked back outside.

She had started to leave, when she spied some candy bars on the picnic table near the lantern. She glanced back at the family. They were busy eating and listening to the story. Before she was even aware of what she was doing, her feet moved forward, and her hand snatched a candy bar.

She had started to move back when she knocked over a thermos.

"What was that?" the boy asked.

"Bears!" his sister yelled.

Jimena bolted into the forest and kept running until she could no longer hear their voices. Then she slid into the clothes she had taken, grateful for the warmth spreading through her. Finally, she unwrapped the candy and took a bite. She held the chocolate on her tongue and let it melt, then leaned against a tree and glanced up.

The moon rose over the treetops, casting a pearly glow on everything around her. The lunar rhythms flowed through her, and her confidence grew. Sunday night the moon was full. The Daughters were strongest then. She felt certain she would be able to save her friends.

But then the premonition of her death intruded, and she stared up at the stars, so clear in the mountain sky, and felt a heaviness in her heart. She had always dared death to take her when it seemed distant, but now it hovered in the near future patiently waiting for her. She closed her eyes and prayed to whatever controlled the universe. She didn't want to die and leave all this beauty.

CHAPTER NINE

B Y THE TIME JIMENA was back in Los Angeles, it was full dark. The moon rode high overhead, and wispy clouds drifted around it. She climbed out of a yellow Ford Pinto.

"Thanks for the ride."

Jimena walked up to Catty's front porch, cursing Chris for ditching her so far from L.A. She was chilled to the bone in spite of the clothing she had stolen, and had spent the last hour in conversation with a man who loved disco music and Cher. The evening could not get worse. All she wanted to do now was take a hot shower, then tell Catty everything, and sleep.

She stepped across the porch and knocked. "Please be home."

The light turned on and the door opened. Catty stood in front of her, looking surprised. Her jeans were pulled down low, exposing her stomach, which was barely covered by a baby T. Her brown hair was tied on her head in a mass of curls.

"I thought you were in San Diego." She held the door open for Jimena to enter.

"I'm there, too."

Catty stared at her. "What happened to you?" She pulled back. "You smell!"

Jimena stomped inside, her anger rising. "You brought me back from the future. That's what happened to me."

"The tunnel did this to you?" Catty closed the door.

"Not the tunnel. You! You were so anxious to go back to the future that you didn't wait to make sure I was close enough to the ground. So you dropped me from about eight feet into the middle of Wilshire Boulevard traffic. I'm lucky to be alive."

Catty stared at her wide-eyed.

"Then I told you not to drop me in enemy territory, and that's exactly where you left me! I almost got killed."

"But you have pine needles and bugs in your hair. How did—"

"I ended up in the mountains." She started to tell her about Chris, but stopped. "It's a long story. You should have been more careful."

Catty burst out laughing.

"It's not funny," Jimena snapped.

Catty held her sides. "Vanessa put you up to this, didn't she?" she said between her giggles.

"What!" Jimena picked up the can of soda that Catty had been drinking and finished it.

"Vanessa got you to do this to pay me back for all the pranks I've played on her. You came back from San Diego early for Corrine's party, didn't you? And Vanessa thought it would be funny to make me think that I had brought you back from the future and screwed things up."

Jimena glared at her.

Catty stopped laughing and stared at Jimena. "Tell me it's a joke."

"Call me." Jimena picked up the cordless phone and handed it to her. "You know the number for my uncle's restaurant in San Diego. Call it and ask to speak to me."

Catty pressed in the number. A fine tremor ran through her fingers now.

Someone answered on the other end.

"Could I speak to Jimena, please?" Catty said. She waited a moment, then her mouth opened and the phone fell from her hand.

Jimena picked it up and listened to her own voice on the other end of the line before hanging up.

With a start Jimena realized she now had two lives going at the same time; the one in San Diego and this new one she was living right now in Los Angeles. The idea made her stomach clench. Catty had always been able to return to the future where she belonged, but Jimena didn't have that power. If she couldn't join her split selves back together, would she live the rest of her life in two separate bodies? What would it feel like to be identical twins who not only looked alike but shared the same memories, thoughts, and loves?

Catty sat down on the floor next to the jeans she had been customizing with sequins and paint. "Don't leave out a detail. Something had to be really bad for me to bring you back and not stay."

Jimena nodded and sat next to her. "You didn't want to come back, but I made you. It was our only hope—"

A loud thumping sound came from the kitchen. "What was that?" Jimena asked.

"The neighbor's cat is always sneaking into the house. I'd better check." Catty rose to see, but before she could go, Jimena stopped her and motioned to her to be quiet.

"What?" Catty asked.

"Do you hear sirens?"

Catty shrugged. "This is Los Angeles."

Jimena stood and crossed the living room to the front window. She stared out at an angle so that she remained hidden. "The police are chasing me."

"Did I cause that, too?" Catty joined her, peering over her shoulder.

Jimena shook her head. "They think I was dealing Ecstasy."

The street looked empty, but the sound of approaching sirens grew louder, and then the first police car turned down the street. Its siren stopped and the pulsing blue lights went out. The car parked in Catty's front drive. A second squad car rolled silently around the corner. The officers from the first one climbed out and headed for the door.

"They must think you did something worse than sell drugs to send so many cars," Catty said softly.

"How could they know I was here?" Jimena looked at Catty.

"Slip out the back." Catty pulled on her arm.

Even as Catty said the words, Jimena had already made her decision. She was going to run. She couldn't chance another night in jail.

"Go." Catty gave her a gentle push. "I'll cover for you."

Jimena hesitated, but her heart had found a faster rhythm, anticipating her flight.

Catty nodded and Jimena slipped from the living room.

A booming knock echoed through the house.

Jimena hurried to the back door but stopped. A manuscript sat on the kitchen table. She leaned over and studied the artwork around the borders of the old parchment. Exotic birds and animals were hidden in the rich patterns of gold, red, and blue. She recognized the miniature of the goddess locking the jaws of hell. This was the Secret Scroll. Why hadn't Catty told her she had found it? Maybe it was what she needed to change the future. Within its ornate calligraphy were instructions for destroying the Atrox. She started to take it, but then remembered the curse. The Scroll had the power to harm anyone who held it. Even Regulators feared it. Only Catty was immune to the sickness it inflicted.

The front door opened, and Catty's muffled voice invited the officers inside.

Jimena had delayed too long. Within seconds the police would be searching through the house. She crossed the kitchen, wrapped her hand around the doorknob, and turned it without making a sound. She eased outside, then sprinted across the wet grass to the redwood fence, grabbed the top, and scaled it.

As she dropped into the next yard, the gate creaked open behind her. She peered back through the slats. Two officers walked across Catty's patio, shining their flashlights over the potted plants.

A cold sweat broke across her forehead as she realized how close she had come to being caught. She turned and studied the unfamiliar yard. A light from the kitchen shone across the grass. She wondered which way to go. She listened for sounds of movement and wished she had Serena's ability to press her mind into the night and see with her thoughts, or Vanessa's power to become invisible and float away. Catty's gift would have been the best right now. With it, she could have escaped in time and returned to a happy memory. Even Tianna's ability to move things would have been a help to her.

Finally, she stood and crept along the edge of the lawn, grateful for the quiet jail-issue slippers. At the end of the yard she pushed open the gate and peered out, looking both ways. When she didn't see anyone, she eased into the alley and rested near a lawn mower and a rake.

She tried to concentrate on getting away, but other thoughts kept filling her mind. She didn't understand why Catty hadn't told her about the Secret Scroll. Catty was the heir to the manuscript. Chris would have given it to her if he had found it again. Did that mean Chris had lied to her about no one knowing he was back? Maybe the two of them were hiding something. She wondered if it had anything to do with what had happened Sunday night.

Footsteps crunched the gravel at the far end of the alley. She glanced back. A policeman was walking toward her. She froze. He hadn't seen her yet. She darted under the overhanging branches of a honeysuckle.

From her hiding place, she watched the beam of the flashlight coming closer. If she didn't leave soon, she'd be discovered.

One house down, she saw a walkway near the garage. If she could get to it without being seen, then maybe she could get away.

She stepped from her cover, feeling totally exposed, and walked quickly, her legs trembling beneath her. Her heartbeat pulsed in her vision. She had never felt this kind of fear when she had been ganged-up and on a mission.

A dog barked behind her, startling her.

And then she smiled. The sudden noise was also a cover. She rushed beneath the spreading branches of an orange tree. Oranges fell to the ground and rolled into the weeds. She turned and ran down the walkway at the side of the garage.

Heavy footfalls echoed in the alley behind her. The officer was chasing her now. She sprinted to the front yard and into the street. Her feet slammed the ground, dry breath tore into her lungs. She jumped over a small picket fence and ran to the edge of the house, then stopped in the darkness beneath a bougainvillea. She was certain she could not be seen from across the street. She waited, crouching low, and stared out at the night.

The officer ran to the curb, stopped, and looked both ways.

Cautiously, she stood and crept to the back of the house and into the next alley. She started walking around an electrical pole, when the soft clap of footsteps made her pause. Another officer was walking down this alley, the light of her flashlight exploring trash bins and weeds.

Jimena turned back into the yard, but stopped abruptly. The policeman who had been chasing her was walking down the driveway from the front of the house. She was trapped now. She crouched behind a pile of rags next to a storage shed and pressed back into the straggly branches of an untrimmed rosebush, her breathing so labored she could taste the fragrance of the blossoms.

In minutes, a light would shine on her, but

instead of surrendering she crouched lower and pulled a newspaper around her. She had no choice but to try. It wasn't just for herself. Others were depending on her.

Then the rags in front of her made a sound. A homeless man raised up on an elbow, his lint-filled beard touching the ground. A slow guttural sound came from his mouth.

Running footsteps filled the night. The officers met and shone their flashlight beams on him.

"Shut the lights off," the man yelled, his breath smelling of alcohol. "Can't a guy get any rest around here?"

Jimena froze. One of her pantlegs was exposed. Her heart thundered so loudly, she was sure they could hear it. She closed her eyes and pressed back, thorns sticking into her spine.

"Are you all right, sir?" The policeman stepped closer.

"Why wouldn't I be?" The man nodded and pulled his blanket over his head.

The officers turned and started walking away, speaking in low voices.

Jimena leaned back against the fence, catching her breath, and waited until she could no longer hear them, then, bending low, she stepped over the sleeping man.

His hand shot out and grabbed her ankle.

Sudden terror seized her. If he called for the police, she wouldn't have the energy to outrun them a second time.

CHAPTER TEN

JIMENA YANKED HER foot from the man's grip. His fingers trembled in the air, then he rolled back, a snore escaping his lips.

She watched the end of the alley, listening for hurried footsteps, but the night remained silent. Slowly, she began trudging through the weeds near the fence under the cover of over-hanging trees and bushes. She didn't understand how the police had known she'd be at Catty's. She had wanted to spend the night there, but now she couldn't go back. And if the police had so easily found her, then it wasn't safe for her to stay with other friends or her grandmother. Maybe she could go downtown and blend in with the homeless people who set up camp every night near the flower market.

Then another idea came to her. Cops didn't go looking for you in the home of your enemy. Payasa would be out with her homies until dawn, and everyone knew her parents worked nights at LAX. Jimena started walking.

Less than an hour later, Jimena moved stealthily under the shadows of palm trees and cottonwoods. This neighborhood belonged to Wilshire 5, Payasa's gang. Gray-blue lights from televisions flickered in the front windows of the small wood-enhouses facing the street.

Running steps slapped the sidewalk behind her. She slipped in back of a thicket of oleander bushes and waited. The footfalls grew louder, and then a man with a collie ran past her.

Relieved, she eased back to the sidewalk.

At the next corner, she passed a *descanso*, a memorial. Pictures of a young boy taped to the lampost fluttered in the night breeze above candles, flowers, stuffed animals, and letters. Flames stretched against the tall glass candleholders, leaving a trail of black soot on the sides. A terrible grief came over her as she stared down at the smiling face in a school photograph.

After a moment, Jimena hurried down to Payasa's house, wanting nothing more than to rest.

The porch light cast an amber glow across the neat flower beds bordering the lawn. She darted to the side of the house, climbed over a wire mesh fence and into the backyard, then hurried toward the patio.

She stumbled over a long chain snaking across the lawn from a huge doghouse. WOLF was painted over the entrance. Payasa hadn't had a dog back when they had played together, but the patio looked the same as Jimena remembered it.

She hurried across the cement slab and pressed against the door, listening for any sounds inside, then she bent down, lifted the doormat, and picked up the key. Jimena smiled to herself, remembering the times she had come home with

Payasa in elementary school. The few times her mother hadn't been there, they had found the key under the mat.

Now Jimena set it into the keyhole, turned the latch bolt, and stole inside to the kitchen. The air was warm and filled with the lingering smells of onions and chilies.

"Hello!" Jimena called out, as if she belonged there, and braced herself in case a dog came leaping at her. She was certain no one was home, but she didn't want any surprises. She glanced at the clock on the stove. The green numbers read 8:15. It was early still. That gave her at least six hours to rest, maybe more.

She hurried down the dark hallway, the tips of her fingers brushing the wall to guide her. Finding a bathroom, she slipped inside, slid a dead bolt in place, and took a deep breath. Jimena turned on the light, and caught her reflection in the medicine cabinet mirror. Pine needles stuck out of her hair and in the red sweater. Black insect specks covered her face.

She pushed the plug into the bathtub drain,

then turned the spigots, and poured peachy bubble bath into the rumbling water.

When she finally slipped into the tub, she thought about her premonition. She leaned back, wondering how her death would affect Collin. Would he still dream of her, think of her . . . love her? Jimena closed her eyes, wondering if she would be able to visit him in spirit. She pictured him now moving about his room, restless for the sun to rise so he could catch the morning waves. Would he be able to feel her hovering nearby?

Just thinking about him ignited a warm joy inside her. She needed to see him and feel his arms around her one last time. Hot tears pressed into her eyes. She didn't want to say good-bye.

A noise made her sit up. She was certain she had heard something that sounded like a door opening. She slipped from the tub, water dripping from her body, and listened. She flicked off the light in case someone had come home, then yanked the robe from the hook on the back of the door and wrapped it around her. She didn't hear anything now. Maybe it had only been the sound of wind rattling against a loose window.

She sighed. She needed to sleep. She left the bathroom and headed toward one of the bedrooms. She entered and quietly closed the door behind her, then with her hands stretched out in front of her, walked across the dark room to the bed. She touched the nightstand, then fell back across the mattress, slamming down on two bodies.

"What the—!"

She jumped back up and switched on a pink lamp.

Payasa stood on the opposite side of the bed, wearing a long T-shirt and white kneesocks, a look of astonishment and rage on her face. A large German shepherd stood beside her, barking ferociously and ready to lunge. Payasa grabbed the red bandanna tied around the dog's neck, then scanned Jimena's hands to see if she had a gun.

Jimena suspected she was frowning, but she didn't know for sure. Payasa had washed her face, and without her eyebrows penciled in, she had a peculiar bald look. A red cut blazed in the middle of her forehead where the sight of her gun had recoiled and hit her.

Jimena grinned. "Was that your first time out with a gun?"

Payasa fingered her forehead, embarrassed, then her anger returned. "Why did they let you out of County?"

"They didn't. I became invisible and flew away."

"I'm sick of your *chistes*. You think you're so funny. Try this." She released her hold on Wolf.

The dog streaked across the bed in a fierce charge, teeth bared. Jimena backed into the corner, knocking over the lamp. It fell to the rug, making shadows shoot at odd angles across the floor and ceiling.

Jimena jerked down the sleeves of the robe to protect her fingers.

Wolf jumped against her, his forepaws thumping on her chest, his hot breath puffing in her face. She banged her head against the wall.

Payasa reached for her cell phone.

"Don't call the cops," Jimena yelled, searching her mind for a lie that could convince Payasa to help her.

"I'm no *rata*," Payasa answered. "I'm calling my homegirls."

"Don't," Jimena yelled, looking for another lie. "I came here to warn you."

Payasa whistled and Wolf backed down, growling deep in his throat, his eyes fixed on Jimena.

Jimena remained against the wall.

"Warn me about what?" Payasa's finger hesitated on the SEND button.

"One of your homegirls is setting you up," Jimena lied.

"Mentirosa." Payasa pushed the button. "Now I know you're a druggie. None of my homegirls would ever rat me out. I know them like I know myself." She made a fist and pounded her chest over her heart.

Suddenly, Wolf stopped growling and whimpered. His ears rotated as if he heard something strange. He tilted his head, whining, and lifted his nose into the air, nostrils flaring, trying to catch the scent of whatever he sensed.

"What did you do to him?" Payasa demanded, and set the phone down.

Jimena raised a hand to quiet her, aware of a mysterious change in the air.

"What?" Payasa asked angrily.

Wolf snorted and shook his head, then licked his muzzle as if something had confused him. His muscles tensed, and his fur bristled.

"If you hurt him I'll—" Payasa stopped speaking and turned as though she felt something odd, too.

Jimena stepped away from the wall and stroked Wolf behind his ears. He licked her hand, suddenly her friend.

Payasa glanced at Jimena, her look of triumph now replaced by one of fear. "Is this more of your *brujita* magic?" She tried to sound tough and dangerous, but her voice trembled.

The edge of the bedspread ruffled as if a sudden draft had crept under the door. Then the large red-and-yellow paper flowers in the green vase on the dresser began to quake.

Wolf began to tremble.

"Dime," Payasa said. "What is it?"

Jimena held out her hand to Payasa. *"Ven.* Come over here with me."

Payasa crawled across the bed and took Jimena's hand. "Are you doing this?"

Jimena shook her head.

A shrill music like the singing of ancient instruments filled the room as a red mist grew in the air.

Payasa took a sharp breath.

The vapor pulled together, becoming a solid form. Great golden wings brushed lazily back and forth, making Payasa's framed pictures of dead homeboys vibrate against the wall.

Payasa gripped Jimena's hand tightly. *"Dios te salve, Maria, llena. . . ."* she whispered, reciting the Hail Mary.

Lizelle materialized. Her dangerous green eyes looked around the room, and then she saw Jimena. Zonda and Azera became whole beside her, their scales shimmering in the odd cast of light.

Jimena knew she shouldn't look, but she was captivated by their unnatural beauty. She attempted to take a step backward, pulling Payasa with her, but her feet had become too heavy to lift. She tried to summon her power, but something stopped it. Were they turning her to stone again?

CHAPTER ELEVEN

WOLF SNARLED AND leaped at the nymphs. His forepaws hit Azera. She pitched backward, trying to hold her balance, then dropped to the floor, flat on her back. Her gossamer wings folded around her. The dog bounded over her, his hind paws tromping across her face as he lunged at Lizelle and Zonda. He snapped at the tips of their lustrous wings. Shrill screams filled the room.

Jimena broke free from Lizelle's spell. She grabbed Payasa's hand and started toward the door.

Payasa jerked back and tried to whistle for

Wolf, but the sound died on her lips. "Com 'ere, boy," she yelled at last, her voice quivering with fear.

Wolf ignored her and pounced on Lizelle. She slapped her long talons at his head, her eyes afire. He jumped back, but then viciously attacked again, his growl low and more menacing than before.

"Now!" Jimena yanked Payasa behind her and ran from the bedroom, down the hallway toward the front of the house. She darted into the living room too quickly and knocked over a lamp. The pottery base shattered, scattering shards across the wood floor. She threw open the door. It banged against the wall, the vibration knocking over tiny crystal angels perched on the TV.

Jimena and Payasa charged across the porch, jumped the three front steps to the sidewalk and took off, tramping through a row of flowering azaleas in the neighboring yard.

Wolf barked madly behind them.

"He'll be all right," Jimena said, trying to reassure Payasa.

A light went on in the neighbor's house and the curtain pulled aside as if someone were peeking out at them.

"Cuidado." Payasa pulled Jimena back. "We have to be more careful. If we're running down the street someone's going to call the cops, or worse, think we don't belong in this neighborhood."

They walked cautiously now, two phantom forms clinging to the darkness flowing beneath the trees. The cold night circled around them. Every fluttering breeze made them pause and study the air. Jimena pulled the robe tightly around her.

After they had gone three blocks, they eased into a driveway, carefully stepping around a stroller and a tricycle, then from behind the corner of the house they peered back at the street.

The porch light shed a dim glow across the front lawn. A sprinkler had been forgotten and left on.

"What are they?" Payasa asked, her respiration jagged.

"Nymphs." Jimena rubbed her chest, trying to ease her racing heart.

"You mean like spirits who live in the woods?" Her voice sounded doubtful. "That can't be. They have to be some kind of government project, like human cloning that went way wrong."

"Nymphs," Jimena repeated. "Let's find a place to hide."

Tall Arizona cypress lined the backyard. The moon cast a milky glow over a child's swing set and the white plastic chairs on the lawn.

"Over there." Jimena pointed to velvet shadows against the fence.

They walked across the wet grass to the side of the yard, then crawled behind the twisted branches of a sprawling juniper bush. The dank smell of dirt wrapped around them.

"Do you think we lost them?" Payasa asked.

Jimena started to nod, but an odd flurry of papers from the trash can made her pause. The small hairs on the back of her neck stood on end as the air took on a palpably charged feeling.

Sprigs of grass whirled in circles, then the

glider and swings began to move back and forth with odd creaking sounds.

"*Madre de Dios*," Payasa muttered.

Suddenly, the dogs in the yard next door erupted in a cacophony of yelps, barks, and howls. Their paws pounded against the redwood fence, making it shake against Jimena's back.

All at once, glistening gold specks sailed around the yard, casting a strange illumination over the trees and bushes. Drops of water reflected the eerie light and sparkled like jewels, giving the night a fairy-tale look.

The nymphs hovered a few inches above the lawn, more apparition than solid form.

"It's like a *pesadilla*," Payasa whispered. "A nightmare, only it's real."

Lizelle fluttered to their hiding place and became solid. The sweep of her wings made the needlelike leaves scrape back and forth across their faces. Her talons brushed aimlessly through the evergreen shrub. Tiny blue-gray berries fell to the ground around them. One of her claws caught a lock of Payasa's hair. Payasa sucked in air and started to scream, but Jimena grabbed her before she could, and pressed her hand over Payasa's mouth.

"We're safe as long as she can't see us," Jimena whispered into her ear.

Payasa nodded. Jimena released her, then turned and stared at Lizelle's shimmering scales through the branches.

A sweet murmur came from Lizelle, as if she were communicating with the others in some ancient song. Jimena sensed disappointment in the tone and wondered if Lizelle had failed in some duty and was afraid to return home.

By some shiver of intuition, Jimena knew that something powerful had directed the nymphs to find her. She was certain that same force had also sent the police earlier, first to the Angeles Forest, and then to Catty's house. Maybe the Atrox had followed her back in time after all and was now playing some cosmic cat-and-mouse game with her.

Abruptly, the nymphs turned and ambled to the front of the house.

"It's okay now," Jimena said with assurance. "They're leaving."

"How do you know?" Payasa seemed doubtful.

"I just do." Jimena crept from their hiding place. She waited for Payasa, then they eased to the front of the house and cautiously peered out at the neighborhood.

Lizelle ran down the street, her giant wings flapping. The downstroke created a freakish wind. Flowers and bushes bent to the ground. Potted plants fell from porch railings and shattered on the sidewalks. Windows rattled and gates creaked as she soared into the sky.

Zonda and Azera followed after her, their gold scales gleaming as they sailed into the air, their wingspans enormous. Their melancholy cries swept through the night like some arcane melody from another time.

Jimena stepped forward and watched them glide overhead.

Porch lights turned on up and down the street. Screen doors opened, and people in robes and pajamas trundled outside.

Jimena and Payasa continued to gaze at the high-flying nymphs. Their bodies dissolved into a reddish gold vapor and then they were gone, leaving only a dazzling rainbow trail across the night sky.

Payasa looked overwhelmed and in shock. "Nymphs," she said incredulously. "How can that be?"

Jimena stared at her for a long time, wondering if she dared tell her the truth. In fourth grade Payasa had read books on mythology. She might even be a help now.

"Did you ever wonder why I quit banging?" Jimena asked.

Payasa nodded. "*Claro*, everyone wanted to know."

"I quit because I found out what I really am." Jimena started walking.

Payasa found an easy pace beside her. "So *dime*, what are you?"

"I'm a goddess—"

"You and your jokes." Payasa shook her head.

"I'm serious," Jimena continued. "I'm a Daughter of the Moon."

Payasa stopped and stared at her, then her eyes slowly widened and a grim smile stretched over her lips. "You're telling me the truth, aren't you?"

"I'm fighting an ancient evil called the Atrox," Jimena explained.

"I've never heard of an Atrox." Payasa began to shiver.

"You remember the story about Pandora?" Jimena asked.

"Yeah." Payasa folded her arms over her chest to warm herself. "Pandora was the one who opened up a storage jar and freed pests and diseases. The Greeks blamed her for all the bad things in the world, because before she lifted the lid, food was everywhere and people didn't have to work to feed themselves."

Jimena nodded. "The last thing to leave the storage vessel was—"

"Hope," Payasa said, finishing her sentence.

"But there's more to the story," Jimena went on. "Something not included in the myth. Selene—"

"The goddess of the moon," Payasa added quickly.

"She saw a creature sent by the Atrox to devour hope. She took pity on humankind and gave her Daughters so they could be guardian angels to perpetuate hope." Jimena spoke softly. "I'm one of those Daughters."

"That's why they're after you?"

"The Atrox and its Followers have sworn to destroy me and my friends."

"There's more of you?" Payasa grabbed Jimena's hand, her palm was cold and sweating.

"Yes," Jimena answered. "Once we're gone, the Atrox will destroy humankind."

"So the nymphs are Followers?"

Jimena shook her head. "No. I'm sure they're just nymphs. They don't have the powers of Followers."

Payasa nervously combed her fingers through her hair. "Followers have more power than what I just saw the nymphs do?"

"The powerful ones do. They could have sensed us hiding in the bushes."

"*No puedo creerlo.*" Payasa looked up at the night sky, shaking her head. "I can't believe it even though I've seen it." She paused as if considering. "I think we should go get my homegirls and destroy them."

"No," Jimena said simply. "I have a better plan. We'll find my friend Serena. Maybe she'll know what's going on." She didn't say her real reason for wanting to go to Serena's house. She needed to see Collin, Serena's brother, and feel his arms around her once more. She closed her eyes, wondering if she should tell him about her premonition.

"*¿Qué te pasa?*" Payasa asked. "Are you okay?"

Jimena nodded. "Just thinking. Come on."

They started walking boldly down the street, then glanced at each other and started laughing.

"We can't catch a bus dressed like this." Jimena pulled at the tie strings on her robe.

Payasa lifted the hem of her T-shirt and stared down at her dirt-stained socks. Her laughter was explosive, but there was a false joy in her outburst. Without warning, her arms were around

Jimena and she was sobbing. Jimena patted her back, knowing she was releasing the tension that had built up inside her.

Finally, Payasa pulled back, wiping her eyes.

"We need a ride," Jimena said. "Do you know someone who's got a car we can use?"

Payasa thought. "Yeah, Slinky always leaves keys in his car in case he's got to make a quick get-away."

"You think he'll let us use it?" Jimena asked.

Payasa nodded, seeming self-confident again, and started walking in the opposite direction.

Minutes later, they were staring at a styling 1956 Chevy parked under a carport.

"He's going to mind like crazy if we take his car." Jimena shook her head, knowing how guys felt about their bombs. She opened the passenger's-side door. The interior was upholstered in blue and purple velvet with diamond tucks.

"I'll call him later." Payasa slid behind a chrome-plated steering wheel and closed the door, then pulled down the driver's-side visor. The keys fell into her lap. She grabbed them, turned one in the ignition, then threw the car into gear and backed out. The rear bumper bounced against the street.

"Be careful," Jimena yelled. The car was low to the ground, and she didn't want some guy coming after them because they had messed up his hydraulic system.

Payasa laughed. "Don't sweat it. He owes me." She changed gears and started forward.

They sped around the corner, the car muffler rumbling against the pavement, and headed west on Wilshire Boulevard. Streetlights reflected off the polished hood and its chrome ornament.

"So where are we going? Mount Olympus?" Payasa seemed too lighthearted now. Jimena knew she was trying to veil her fear with humor.

"Take La Brea North."

They drove in silence for a while, then Payasa switched on the radio and sang with a song, snapping her fingers. She seemed almost buoyant.

"I remember how much you used to read. Do you still?" Jimena asked.

Payasa switched off the radio. "I don't have time. I'm living the life."

"We used to call you *cantadorita* because you were always telling us stories." Jimena felt a sudden sadness, wondering what had happened to the girl she had known in fourth grade. "Graciela—"

Her head jerked around. "Don't call me that. I'm Payasa now."

Jimena clutched her elbow. "Why did you get ganged up?"

Payasa settled back in her seat. Her mood suddenly turned somber.

"You were always the best student," Jimena went on. "All of us thought you'd be famous some day."

"Yeah, the district was going to send me to one of those special schools for kids who are good in math and science, but then . . ." She glanced out the driver's-side window as if reliving some memory. When her eyes came back, she stared at the road ahead. "Lara and I thought it would be fun to go hang out with some kids who were ditching school and having a party."

"Everybody does that once." Jimena shrugged.

Payasa nodded. "But it felt too good, you know, not having to worry about rules or home-work. We didn't go home that night, and then in the morning, we got scared, wondering what our parents would do to us when we did go home. So we didn't. We just stayed away."

"How long?" Jimena asked quietly.

"A week . . . two weeks, long enough so that by the time I did go back, I was ganged up and I didn't even hear my mom screaming at me. Nothing she said could hurt me anymore, because I had my homies and they were my *familia* from then on."

"You ever think about quitting the life?" Jimena asked.

"It's *por vida*," Payasa answered, but Jimena could feel her bitterness and regret.

"Over here." Jimena pointed to Serena's house.

Payasa parked under a large spreading mag-nolia, then turned off the motor.

Jimena joined her outside on the smooth lawn and stared up at the two-story Spanish-style home. Plum trees heavy with blossom rustled lazily in the night breeze.

"It doesn't look like anyone's home," Payasa said. "What do you want to do?"

Jimena studied the dark windows, wondering where Serena and Collin had gone. She wanted to tell Collin about her premonition now. He always knew the right words to comfort her. She needed to feel his warm hands stroking her hair, her lips kissing the top of her head as she cradled against him. "I think we'll go inside and wait."

"Good." Payasa started up the stone walkway. "I'm freezing."

They ducked under a huge bougainvillea that trailed up the side to the house and continued down the drive to the back.

Jimena opened the door.

"They leave the house unlocked?" Payasa asked, unable to keep the surprise from her voice.

Jimena flicked on a light. "Don't get any ideas."

Payasa followed her into the yellow kitchen and walked over to the cello resting behind a silver music stand in the corner. She flicked a string. A single note resounded.

"Serena plays the cello." Jimena walked over to the sink and grabbed a glass. "Do you still play the violin?"

Payasa shook her head and joined Jimena. "I killed *mami*'s dreams of seeing me in a big mariachi contest someday."

"You were cute in your *traje de charro*," Jimena said. "You looked like a fancy horsewoman in your jacket and that long black skirt with the silver decorations up the side."

Payasa shrugged. "I better call Slinky and let him know we have his car." She walked over to the phone on the counter and punched in a number.

"Jimena?" a deep voice called from the hallway.

Jimena turned abruptly.

Collin stood behind her. His white-blond hair fell across his tan forehead. She took a deep breath, loving the way he looked.

"Are you all right?" He walked toward her.

There was real concern in his blue eyes, but something else she couldn't read.

"You can't imagine everything that's happened." She fell against him and slipped her arms around his waist. His body radiated delicious warmth. She breathed the spicy smell of his aftershave and let her hands slide up his back. She hadn't realized until now how much she had longed for the comfort of his embrace. She parted her lips in sweet anticipation and leaned back, waiting for his kiss.

He cleared his throat and stepped away from her, arms at his sides.

"What's wrong?" she asked, baffled.

"I just tried to call you in San Diego." He looked confused. "Your brother told me you were working. Now you're standing in front of me barely dressed in a bathrobe." His eyes dropped and moved over her body, then as if he were embarrassed, he looked up, and a blush rose beneath his tan.

"I am down in San Diego." Jimena adjusted the robe around her. "But I'm here, too. Catty brought me back from the future. I need to talk to Serena about—"

"Serena's at Corrine's party," he answered too abruptly.

For the first time Jimena noticed that Collin was dressed in khaki pants and a black T-shirt. He usually hung out in sweats or baggy shorts. Did that mean he had been planning to go to the party without her?

Before she could ask him, he spoke. "Get something to wear out of Serena's closet and I'll take you to the party so you can talk to her."

"Okay." Jimena hesitated. She had so much more she had wanted to tell him. She needed his warmth and understanding.

"Hurry," he urged.

Payasa slammed the receiver down. Collin glanced up, as if seeing her for the first time.

"My friend Payasa," Jimena said.

"Hey." Collin nodded.

"Did you tell Slinky?" Jimena asked.

"I left him a message," she answered, smiling at Collin.

Jimena walked toward the hallway. "Come on."

"Where?" Payasa followed after her.

"We're going to get ready for a party," Jimena answered over her shoulder and started up the stairs. When she reached the top of the stairwell, she paused and leaned over the handrail, trying to see Collin. Why hadn't he seemed happy to see her?

"What now?" Payasa asked nervously.

"Nothing." Jimena continued to Serena's room. She switched on the overhead light.

"*Mírame.*" Payasa caught her reflection in the dressing-table mirror. "Look at me." She sat down, grabbed black eyeliner, and started to draw in an eyebrow.

Jimena tapped her shoulder. "Maybe you should wear your makeup different."

Payasa paused. "What do you mean?"

"Do you really think you got your nickname from the way you're always fooling around and telling jokes?" Jimena asked.

Payasa stared at her.

"I'm serious." Jimena took the liner away from her, then picked up a brown pencil and feathered in eyebrows. "The way you do it, you look like you have two scared snakes racing over your forehead. Doesn't this look better?"

Payasa shrugged.

"You know it does." Jimena took a dark gray eyeliner and outlined Payasa's upper and lower lashes, then used a slate-gray powder to smudge on color. When she finished, Payasa had a smoldering look.

"Wow," Payasa whispered, staring at herself in the mirror.

"You'd better get something to wear." Jimena pointed to Serena's huge walk-in closet. "That T-shirt won't do it."

Payasa found sandals with leather flowers and string ties. She held them up. "What would my homies think if they saw me in these?"

Jimena pulled on a slinky skirt, then picked up sandals with delicate rhinestone buckles. She started to step into the shoes when a sound made her turn.

Payasa was ripping out the waistband from a pair of jeans.

"What are you doing?" Jimena asked.

"I got to make them low-slung," Payasa explained, biting at a thread with her teeth.

"But they're already hip-huggers," Jimena pointed out. "They'll be so low your butt will show every time you sit down."

Payasa smiled wickedly. "I don't plan on being a wallflower."

Jimena shook her head, then slipped into an electric-pink halter top and looked in the mirror, admiring her bare midriff. She loved the way the silky material whispered against her skin.

Payasa stepped into the jeans, then pulled on an off-the-shoulder top with swirls of sequins. She stared at her reflection and laughed. "I have some serious elegance here."

"Come on." Jimena started from the room. "It's time for you to go break some hearts."

Downstairs, they paraded in front of Collin. Jimena knew she looked fine, so why wasn't

Collin showing his appreciation? He seemed preoccupied. Even his smile looked tense. Then she remembered that he had been trying to call her in San Diego.

"What were you going to tell me on the phone?" she asked.

"It's not important now." Collin shook the car keys in his hand. "Let's go to the party."

Jimena pulled him to the far side of the kitchen. "You keep acting like something big is bothering you. Tell me what it is." She let her hands slide up his arms and pressed her body closer to his.

"I'm going to wait for you outside," Payasa said, and left.

Collin stared at Jimena and slipped his hands into his pockets. His silence made her nervous.

"I think we should start seeing other people," he said finally.

She tried to swallow, but her throat had become too dry. Her stomach tensed, and she took slow deep breaths. She pulled her hands back and let them fall rigid at her sides.

"Is it because we never . . . because we didn't . . ."

He shook his head. "I've always respected your decision not to do that."

"Then what?"

"I just think it's better." His jaw muscles clenched.

"All right." She nodded, pushing back her emotions. She hated the empty, achy feeling spreading through her. "I knew you had been acting distant lately, but I never thought it was this bad."

"We can still be friends." He tried to smile and started toward the door as if nothing had happened between them.

"Friends?" Anger awakened inside Jimena. It was all she could do to keep her hands at her sides. She wanted to pick up a chair and throw it.

"Coming?" he asked without turning back to look at her.

She waited until she knew she had her voice under control. "You go on. We have our own wheels."

He cleared his throat, then turned in the doorway. "You sure?"

She gave him a lighthearted grin and stretched her body in a flamboyant tease to show him what he was going to miss. Hiding her pain was something she knew well. "Yeah, see you at the party."

CHAPTER TWELVE

JIMENA AND PAYASA drove into the Hollywood Hills to a dark narrow street overgrown with trees and shrubs. Kids stood on steps leading up to a trilevel house perched next to the slope.

Payasa steered the car to the curb and parked. Immediately guys swarmed around it, admiring the look, their hands smoothing over the bumper and grille.

Guitar-driven hard rock vibrated around them as Jimena and Payasa climbed from the car and headed up the walk. Fragrant gardenias and small lights bordered the gray stepping-stones to the front of the house.

Jimena looked up and down the crowded walkway. The anxiety inside her began to loosen. She didn't think the nymphs or the police would come looking for her here. She felt a rising sense of safety.

She and Payasa walked through the mirrored entrance to a large living room. Furniture had been pushed back against the white walls. Some kids stood around but most were dancing in a tight circle.

"Let's go outside." Jimena motioned to the open patio door.

The DJ had set up next to a trickling waterfall.

Serena stood at the concession. She turned as if she had sensed their presence and waved. She wore a fuchsia tube top with low-slung jeans and two vintage leather belts hanging loosely over her hips. She pushed through the crowd of kids and met them at the patio door.

"I thought you were in San Diego." She had

a breezy playful manner, as if she were in a happy mood.

"Didn't Catty tell you?" Jimena asked.

"I haven't seen Catty," Serena said. "What was she supposed to tell me?"

Serena didn't wait for an answer. She pressed inside Jimena's head. Her large expressive eyes turned anxious. Jimena hid what had happened at the Staples Center because she wanted to tell everyone about it at the same time, but she let Serena see the nymphs and her journey back from the future.

"Is she one?" Payasa whispered against Jimena's ear.

"Yeah, this is Serena."

Serena smiled at Payasa, then turned to Jimena. "Why did you come back from the future?"

Payasa gasped. "Time travel, too?"

Jimena nodded, then she answered Serena's question. "I'll explain when I have all of you together. Right now I'm worried about Catty."

"Maybe Tianna knows where she is. Come on."

They walked over to a wooden floor that had been set up on the grass in the corner of the yard. A group of kids dressed in nylon jackets and hooded sweatshirts stood around a breaking circle, challenging each other and battling over who had the better moves.

Tianna burst into the circle and started popping. Her long silky black hair fell over her shoulders.

"When did Tianna become a b-girl?" Jimena asked.

"She looks like a goddess," Payasa mumbled. "Does she have witch powers, too?"

"Goddess powers," Jimena corrected. "She can move things with her mind."

Tianna bent the tips of her fingers in a wave that curled up her arm to her shoulder, then down her body to her legs in one flowing motion. She did a foot rock, then a backspin, before she jumped up and joined Jimena, Serena, and Payasa. Her skills shocked the guys, who applauded.

"Hey!" Tianna's face looked flushed, as if she were coming down with a fever.

"Great moves," Payasa said.

"Do you know where Catty is?" Serena asked.

"Catty had to work," Tianna said, but her voice seemed guarded, and Jimena wondered why. "I went by her house earlier to pick her up for the party, but she wasn't home. She left a note on the front door, saying she had to work in her mom's store."

"I wanted to talk to you all at once," Jimena said, disappointed.

"About what?" Vanessa joined them. She wore a leather skirt with a short jacket. Her lacy blouse was cut low, showing off the arabesque tattoo over her heart. Her blond hair was smooth and swinging in her face.

"She's one, too." Payasa studied Vanessa. "Does she have a power?"

"You told her about us?" Vanessa looked surprised.

"This is Payasa," Jimena explained. "She was with me when I was attacked."

Vanessa looked concerned, then she smiled at Payasa. "I can go invisible," she told her.

"So what's up?" Vanessa asked. "I thought you were in San Diego."

"I still am," Jimena explained. "My other self is, anyway. The Jimena you're looking at came back from the future."

"Catty brought you back and left you?" Vanessa frowned. "Why didn't she stay?"

"Leaving me was our only hope to find a way to change the future."

"What happened?" Tianna coughed and took a Kleenex from her pocket.

Jimena started to speak, but as her friends gathered close around her, another premonition vibrated through her. Her vision began to blur, and she felt herself detaching from the world. Soon, she was plummeting into that other place deep inside herself.

In this premonition, Vanessa, Catty, Serena, and Tianna stood facing her, but now their smiles panicked her. One of them was wearing a mask and deceiving the others. She tried to push her vision farther to see who it was, but the mental picture kept slipping away, and then it was gone, leaving her with a definite sense that one of her best friends would betray her. Was that what had happened at the Staples Center?

She opened her eyes and stared at the concerned faces of her friends.

"What did you see?" Vanessa asked.

Jimena hesitated.

"What?" Serena coaxed, her eyes anxious.

"One of you is going to betray the rest of us," she said softly.

"Are you sure?" Tianna asked.

"Maybe it's not what it seems," Serena offered. "After all it's not as if you haven't misinterpreted your premonitions before."

"I hope I'm wrong," Jimena answered, but she didn't think she had misunderstood.

Each of the Daughters had a powerful dark side. Vanessa was a Daughter of the Moon, but she was also a Daughter of Pandora. Serena was the key, the one with the power to alter the balance between light and dark, and she was in love with Stanton, a Follower. Catty's father was a powerful member of the Inner Circle, and her birth mother had been a Daughter of the Moon who had turned to the Atrox. Kendra had found Catty walking along an Arizona highway after her real mother had deserted her.

Then Jimena glanced at Tianna. Did she have another side? She hadn't been born a goddess. She had become one later. Jimena didn't really know much about her. Could she be the traitor? She claimed Followers had killed her family, but was that true? How had she gotten her telekinetic powers and her unearthly beauty? Could those be gifts from the Atrox?

"So what were you going to tell us?" Vanessa urged. "What happens in the future?"

Jimena hesitated. "It's better if I wait until I have all of you together." Until she knew which one was deceiving her, she thought it best not to say anything. Any information could inadvertently help the traitor.

Vanessa seemed annoyed. "You came back from the future to warn us about something, and now you're not going to tell us?"

Jimena could feel Serena tickling inside her

mind, searching for the answer. She blocked her, and Serena scowled.

"I'll tell you when we're all together," she said firmly.

The hard-rocking music stopped, and a romantic song started up. The singer's voice felt like a gentle purr.

Michael Saratoga ran over to Vanessa, his full, sensual lips easing into a smile. His wild black hair was moussed into jagged spikes. He had strong angular features and dark, friendly eyes.

"Who's that hottie?" Payasa asked.

"Vanessa's boyfriend," Jimena said. "Don't get any ideas."

Then Derek nodded a greeting. "Hey." His long red hair was pulled back in a ponytail. His deep blue eyes looked lovestruck as he eased Tianna into his arms. She tilted her head and kissed him. They disappeared into the crowd of dancers.

Serena bit her lip and glanced at the shadows in the back of the yard behind the DJ. "See you." She walked away from them.

Jimena knew she was meeting up with Stanton again. Her stomach clenched. Could her best friend be the one who would betray them? She didn't think so. After all, Serena had had too many opportunities to do so before now. But her relationship with Stanton made Jimena worry.

She turned to Payasa. "Let's ditch this place."

"Are you sure?" Payasa asked, scanning the room. "Lots of guys are checking us out."

"Come on."

They pushed through the jammed dance floor. Guys started dancing with them, teasing and not letting them pass. Jimena felt trapped in the moving arms and legs. She glanced at Payasa, who was waving her hands over her head. Finally, she elbowed her way to the door.

Just as she was about to leave, she stopped abruptly. Collin was dancing with another girl. She had curly blond hair and wore a satiny slip dress.

"What's up?" Payasa asked.

Hot jealousy ripped through Jimena. "So soon."

"*¿Mande?*" Payasa asked.

"Look at him," Jimena sneered. "We were going together until just a little while ago. Now he's dancing like he's forgotten my name already."

"Forget him. He's not your type," Payasa assured her.

"You don't know." Jimena watched Collin stroke the girl's glistening hair.

"Why would he want a wimp like that?" Payasa asked. "She looks like a vic."

"Yeah," Jimena agreed. "The opposite of me. I bet she doesn't have a single tattoo on her perfect body."

"You're better."

"Then how come he's with her?" Collin had always told Jimena that he didn't care about her past, but now she wondered.

"Show him he's nothing," Payasa urged.

"Yeah." Jimena started swaying to the beat. She tilted her head, eyes flashing at a guy she recognized from Michael's band. He was tall and dark. His eyes were drawn to her as if by magic.

She slid her hands over her head and kept them there, staring at the good-looking guy, moving her hips with the slow, sultry music.

His eyes lingered, taking in every bit of her, and she let him look.

Payasa shook her head. "I've never seen anyone get the guys the way you can. Is that part of your goddess magic?"

Jimena shook her head. "They're scared of me," she whispered. "Even this one." She nodded slightly and he stepped toward her.

"Want to dance?" he asked, pressing his warm hands on either side of her waist. He was a good dancer. She had seen him before.

"What's your name?" she whispered.

"Robert," he answered. "I know yours. Jimena."

They danced close, hips sensual and easy, his jeans rubbing against her bare thigh.

"You look hot," he whispered. "You always do."

She could feel the jealous stares of other guys, but there was only one she wanted to burn with envy. She edged closer to Robert, easing him back into the dancers.

When they were near Collin, Jimena shot him a quick glance. He stared at her, tight-lipped, his eyes impossible to read.

She nuzzled against Robert. When she looked up again, Collin was walking his new girl to the concession at the edge of the patio.

She stopped dancing.

"What?" Robert asked, pulling back.

"Sorry, I got a sudden headache." She rubbed her forehead.

Robert looked baffled.

"Sorry," she repeated, feeling miserable. She hated to think she was the kind of girl who would use a guy to make another one jealous. She tried to make up excuses for her bad behavior, but she knew what she had done was wrong.

"Do you want me to give you a ride home?" Robert asked.

Payasa came to her rescue. "I'll take her home. I told her she was too sick to come to the party anyway."

Jimena rushed outside before anyone could see her tears. She stood next to a giant wisteria. The graceful flowers fluttered against her as soft as angel wings. She brushed the wetness from her face and tried to convince herself that it was crazy to feel so hurt when she only had a short time to live.

CHAPTER THIRTEEN

"WHERE ARE WE going now?" Payasa asked as she settled in behind the steering wheel.

Jimena stared out the window, her mind racing. Even though Serena was seeing Stanton, she trusted her the most. She didn't want to chance running into Collin, but she wasn't going to be able to avoid him forever. Then another thought came to her, and a grim smile crossed her lips. She wondered if she would be able to come back and haunt him. Could she make him feel how much he had hurt her?

"Let's go back to Serena's house," she said finally.

"Maybe it's better if we keep moving." Payasa didn't bother to hide her uneasiness.

"I don't think the nymphs are coming after us again tonight."

"Why not?" Payasa started the car and they rolled away.

"If the nymphs were going to show up again, they would have found us already," Jimena said with assurance. "Whatever force was telling them where to find me has given up for now."

Payasa nodded. "I could use some sleep."

Jimena studied Payasa. "Why were you home in bed so early tonight? I thought for sure you'd be out with your homies."

"I was." Anger seeped into her voice. "But then Slinky ditched me for this hood rat who snaps to it for the guys."

"So we stole his car to get even?" Jimena asked, dismayed.

"Borrowed it," Payasa corrected.

Jimena shook her head and smiled. "You're some *chica*, Payasa."

"I know."

Twenty minutes later, they parked in the back of Serena's house near the garage. Payasa tucked the keys into the visor as they climbed out.

The glossy leaves had taken on the white luster of moonlight. Jimena spread her arms and let the lunar glow flow through her. The moon had a powerful influence over the oceans, making the waters ebb and rise. She wondered if it really was strong enough to protect her as Maggie, her mentor and guide, had said.

Suddenly, Payasa grabbed Jimena's hand and pointed at a shadow.

"There," she whispered harshly.

An inky silhouette slid over the side of the garage and slipped into the shifting shadows beneath the tree.

Jimena stood in front of Payasa even though she was certain the murky image was only Serena and Stanton.

The air filled with a hissing sigh like air escaping from a tire, and then the darkness ripped open. Two cloudy figures poured from the gloom. Stanton appeared before them, his menacing eyes luminescent. He stepped from the dimness into the moonlight, his eyes glowing yellow.

Payasa sucked in air. "What is he?"

"A Follower," Jimena whispered, feeling his evil aura. She wondered how Serena could care for him so deeply.

Serena stepped from behind him, smiling broadly.

"Why did you guys leave the party so soon?" she asked as if there were nothing unusual about her ghostly arrival. "Did something happen?"

Stanton's long fingers caressed her shoulder. "I'd better go. I think my presence is scaring someone." A wry smile formed on his lips as he glanced at Payasa, then leaned back and dissolved, blending into the night.

"Come on." Serena grabbed Payasa's arm. "Don't be afraid of him."

"People should be afraid of him, Serena," Jimena countered.

Serena acted as if she hadn't heard the comment and hurried inside. She switched on the light. The yellow kitchen felt warm and inviting.

Wally, Serena's pet raccoon, scurried to them, his toenails clicking on the linoleum. She scooped him into her arms and rubbed her face in his fur.

Payasa petted him.

"Get out the ice cream while I feed Wally." Serena set him down. He paced near his water dish, his tail high in the air, while Serena filled a bowl with chunks of apples and a can of cat food.

Jimena took a half-gallon container of rocky road ice cream from the freezer, picked three spoons from a drawer, then sat down at the table. She handed Payasa a spoon, then put one on the table for Serena.

"I know you had a premonition that upset you." Serena joined them with a canister of whipped cream and sprayed it into the carton. "But I can feel other emotions buzzing around you. What's up?"

"Check it out," Jimena said bitterly. "Collin broke up with me."

"I can't believe it." Serena's eyes widened as she dug her spoon into the ice cream. "Did he tell you why?"

Jimena shook her head. "I think he found someone else."

"Some little sweetie," Payasa said with too much anger, as if she were thinking about Slinky again.

"It's odd he didn't tell me." Serena licked her spoon.

"Duh, you're my best friend, do you think he would?" Jimena took two long breaths, trying to calm herself.

Serena dug her spoon back in the carton. "I know he still likes you."

"Did you read his mind?" Jimena asked with sudden hope.

"No," she answered. "You don't need to be

a mind reader to know how crazy he is about you."

Jimena set down her spoon with a soft clank. "I'm getting an ice-cream headache, and I'm exhausated."

"Me, too." Payasa sighed.

"Yeah, let's get some sleep." Serena took the carton and pushed it back in the freezer, then they headed upstairs.

In her bedroom, Serena pulled two sleeping bags from the bottom of her closet and handed Jimena and Payasa each a pair of sweats.

"There's one more thing I've been keeping from you," Jimena started slowly as she unzipped the sleeping bag.

"Yeah?" Serena kicked out of her shoes and stepped into her sweat bottoms.

"I had a premonition of my own death," Jimena confessed.

Payasa turned, stunned. Serena sat on the edge of the bed, her arms locked over her chest as if she were afraid she was going to lose control. Both stared at her.

"It's coming soon," Jimena continued.

Serena stood suddenly and went to her desk. She picked up her tarot deck and started shuffling. "We all know you're not always right in what you think you see."

"I'm right this time, Serena."

"There could be another meaning," she said eagerly. "Let's look at the cards. Maybe we'll get a clue for a different interpretation."

Jimena shook her head slowly. "I know what I saw."

"Let's try." Serena seemed desperate. She held the deck in her hand for Jimena to tap.

When Jimena wouldn't touch it, she sat on the green sleeping bag and shuffled anyway. As she picked up the first card, Jimena grabbed her wrist.

"It's going to be the death card, Serena," Jimena whispered. "Listen to me. I don't have that much time and I need your help."

Serena turned the card. She looked at its face and let it fall to the ground. Tears gathered around the edges of her eyes.

They were silent for a long time, staring at each other, and then Jimena spoke. "I want you to help me plan my funeral."

"No." The word came out a quiet cry. Serena shook her head.

"I want you to play your cello for me at my funeral," Jimena continued. "Something that will make people feel a longing for life, so they'll appreciate what they have."

"Don't talk about it!" Serena shouted. "It's not going to happen. I can't let my best friend go. I won't."

"We've never been able to stop any of my premonitions from coming true," Jimena reminded her.

"We'll find a way this time," Serena said defiantly.

Jimena glanced at Payasa. Their eyes met in understanding. She and Payasa had planned their own funerals a dozen times or more. All homegirls had.

Serena stood, her face tense. "I'm going to take a shower."

She left the room. The bathroom door closed, and then Jimena could hear Serena crying over the steady flow of running water.

Payasa picked up a notebook from the desk and sat down next to Jimena. "Do you have any regrets?" she asked softly.

Jimena nodded. "I wish I knew what loving felt like."

Payasa looked up at her. "You never?"

She shook her head. "I've seen what happens to the girls who snap to it for the guys."

"Yeah." Payasa looked away.

"You?"

"Never. No one's going to catch me sexing a *vato*. I play the game, but I see the way my home-boys treat the girls who do it. I have pride. I don't want to be some *chavala* they kick around like an old can."

"I'll miss you," Jimena said. "I think we could have been good friends again, like we were before."

"Why didn't we stay best friends?" Payasa asked.

"Wilshire Boulevard," Jimena answered.

"It doesn't make sense, you know?" Her face looked puzzled.

"But it does when you're in fifth grade and scared," Jimena whispered. "Fear gets us into a mess of trouble."

Payasa nodded, then she picked up a pen and wrote JIMENA'S FUNERAL in large scrawling letters across the top of the page.

"Dime," she whispered and waited.

"I want to wear my grandmother's wedding dress," Jimena started. "It's about the only thing she brought up with her that night from Mexico. She wanted me to wear it for—" Her voice fell away.

Payasa nodded and wrote it down.

"And play happy music for me. My life wasn't sad. Serena will come around. She'll play something on her cello. She's good."

By the time Serena returned, smelling of strawberry shampoo, Jimena had finished. Payasa tore the papers from the notebook, folded them, and put them in the pocket of her sweatpants.

Serena's eyes were red, her face cheerless. "Maybe we should get some sleep now," she said, already turning off the lights.

Serena and Payasa fell asleep quickly, but Jimena felt too edgy. She kept thinking about Sunday night, the nymphs, and Collin.

Finally, she decided to distract herself with some TV downstairs. She pushed her sleeping bag aside, left the bedroom, and started down the dark hallway. When she passed Collin's room, the door was open. She paused and peered inside. Light from a street lamp fell across his bed and dresser. His room was empty.

She wandered in, picked up his sweater from the bed, and pulled it around her, enjoying the smell of his aftershave. She walked over to his dresser and touched a photo of him down at the beach catching a wave.

Hurried footsteps on the hallway runner made her turn.

The overhead light snapped on. She blinked furiously, trying to make her eyes adjust to the brightness.

Collin walked into the room, unaware of her presence, his hair wet and dripping, a towel slung around his waist. Before she could warn him that she was there, he slammed the door and threw his towel on the bed, then looked up and saw her.

"Dang!" he shouted. "What are you doing in here, Jimena?"

He grabbed the towel and whipped it around him, but not before her eyes had dropped and moved down his body.

Embarrassed, she coughed.

"Jimena?"

For the first time in her life she felt too self-conscious to speak. Her face heated with a blush. If he hadn't liked her before, he was going to hate her now. She ran from the bedroom, brushing against him as she opened the door, and pounded down the stairs, taking them two at a time. At the landing she paused, hoping Collin had chased after her to tell her everything was all right, but the house remained silent.

Catching her breath, she walked into the family room, turned on the TV, wrapped an orange afghan around her, and sprawled on one of the couches. The day could not possibly get worse.

Finally she became drowsy and clicked off the set. She snuggled down and fell into an uneasy sleep. She dreamed of a woman whose face was hidden behind a shimmering blue veil, motioning Jimena to come toward her.

"Who are you?" Jimena whispered, even though part of her knew already.

"I'm Mother Death," the woman answered in a soothing voice. "Lift the veil and see my face."

Jimena trembled. She knew that to see the woman's face was to die. But instead of backing away, she stepped forward, her hand reaching in front of her, and pinched the silky material. The veil fell to the floor.

The dream startled her awake. She sat up with a jolt and rubbed her hand on her chest, trying to calm her racing heart.

In the darkness she heard stealthy footsteps creeping toward her. Had Mother Death stepped from her dream into reality?

She gasped and turned, her eyes searching the unlit room for any movement. She started to swing her legs off the couch to investigate, when a hand clasped over her mouth and pulled her back.

▼

CHAPTER FOURTEEN

JIMENA STRAINED HER neck and looked into Catty's eyes.

She slowly released her hold. "I was afraid I'd startle you, and I didn't want your scream to wake everyone."

"How did you find me here?" Jimena switched on a lamp.

"I knew you'd be with Serena, so I snuck into the house. They really should lock their back door. Anyway, I was starting up the stairs, and I heard someone talking, so I came in here. Who was with you?" Catty glanced around. She was wearing the jeans she had customized earlier with sequins and paint. Glistening waves curled up the pant legs.

"No one was here." Jimena brushed her hands through her hair. "I was dreaming."

Catty kneeled beside the couch. "After the cops left me, I found the Secret Scroll sitting on the kitchen table." She stood suddenly and spread her arms. "Just like that, it appeared. I don't know how it got there."

"You don't?" Jimena asked, surprised. "How could it just appear?"

"At first I'd hoped that Chris had brought it back." She looked down at her hands, and sighed. "It's so obvious I'm still crushing on a guy I'll probably never see again."

"Maybe he'll come back." Jimena wondered if she should tell Catty what she knew.

"Some day," Catty said wistfully. "But I know it couldn't have been Chris, because he has to hand me the Scroll. Someone or something else brought it back. That worried me enough, and now I've lost it!"

"It has to be in your house someplace."

Catty flopped onto the couch. "The night clerk at my mom's store got sick. She called while I was studying the Scroll and asked me to come down to close for her. So I put the Scroll in the cupboard by the stove, or at least I thought I did. Maybe I left it out on the table. I can't remember. I was so rushed and upset. But when I got back, it wasn't there. I've been looking for it ever since, then I thought maybe you had seen it and had come back and taken it."

"There's no reason for me to take it," Jimena answered. "The Scroll's curse almost killed your mother. It's dangerous for anyone except you."

Catty cradled a pillow. "If you didn't take it, then I'm afraid my mom has it. Do you think she'd start translating it again in spite of the curse?"

"Just ask her."

"I did, but then I got to thinking. She wouldn't tell me if she did have it."

"Why wouldn't she tell you?" Jimena

thought about Catty's mother. Kendra knew the truth about all of them, and as a Latin scholar had helped them translate the Secret Scroll when Catty had had it before.

"She'd think this time she'd be able finish the translation before she got too sick." Catty sighed. "She'd do anything to help us."

"Maybe she doesn't have it."

"Then who? It has to be her." Catty raked her fingers through her hair. "What will happen if Professor Hendrix sees the Scroll accidentally? You remember, my mom's boss? He's a world-renowned authority on old manuscripts, and he won't miss a chance to use the Scroll and get his picture on the cover of *Time* magazine."

"Don't worry about it," Jimena tried to comfort her. "Even if he does find it, no one will believe all the stuff it says about the Atrox and the Daughters."

"But if people who are translating it start dying, everyone will know the curse is real, and then maybe they'll start believing the other stuff about us."

Jimena considered what she was saying. "We'll go over to UCLA tomorrow and check out your mom's office so you won't have to worry."

"There's something more." Catty looked as if she were working out a problem.

"What?" Jimena asked, suddenly nervous.

"I'm been trying to go into the future to see if my mom has the scroll, but something is blocking me."

"What do you mean?" Jimena began to tremble. Instinct told her she didn't want to hear what Catty was going to say next.

"I've never found a barricade in the tunnel before. But there's definitely an obstruction now, as if time has stopped. Weird, huh? I can't go into the future past Sunday night."

"Not as weird as you think," Jimena mumbled more to herself than to Catty.

"What?"

"Get some sleep now," Jimena said. "Then tomorrow we'll start looking for the Scroll."

Catty curled onto the other couch, but her

eyes remained open. "I really liked Chris," she said slowly.

When her eyes closed, Jimena turned off the light, and sat on the couch, staring into the dark. She pushed with her power trying to force her mind to see the days ahead.

Maggie had been teaching her how to expand her gift to look into the future without having to wait for a premonition. This new ability was like having memories of events that were waiting for her in the time to come. That made it hard to trust the accuracy of what she saw. A premonition came at her like a brick through a window, but this other kind of perception wasn't as strong.

Usually she could pick up little things that would occur a week or even a month ahead, like spilled milk or rainstorms, but now, like Catty's time travel, her mind seemed blocked. She couldn't go farther than Sunday night. Did that mean she only had two days to live, or could the meaning be worse? Could the future cease to exist after Sunday night?

CHAPTER FIFTEEN

SATURDAY MORNING, Jimena took a cup of coffee out to Serena's backyard. "Slinky's car is gone," she yelled, and hurried back inside to the kitchen.

"I called Slinky again last night and told him where I was." Payasa shrugged and spooned sugar into her coffee. "He must have come over and taken the car back."

"We need wheels." Serena filled a bowl with cereal. "It'll take too much time if we have to catch buses over to UCLA."

Catty sat on the counter in the sunlight cascading through the windows. She set her doughnut down, licked her fingers, and picked up the phone. "I'll get us a ride."

"How?" Serena asked.

"Vanessa." Catty smiled impishly.

"No way." Serena buttered her toast. "You know how she is about rules."

"She won't do it," Jimena agreed. "She just got her driver's license, so it's only provisional. She's not allowed to drive without an adult, and for sure she can't cruise with her friends yet."

"I can talk her into anything," Catty said with assurance and stretched the telephone cord out into the hallway.

A few minutes later she came back into the kitchen. "Okay, Vanessa will be here in a few minutes. We'll pick up Tianna first, then go over to UCLA."

"How did you get her to do it?" Serena asked and tore off a piece of toast for Wally.

"Easy," Catty bragged. "I promised I'd customize three pair of jeans for her."

Within twenty minutes, Vanessa was parked at the curb in a red 1965 Mustang convertible. She honked and waved.

"Where'd she get that car?" Serena asked, not bothering to hide the envy in her voice.

"It used to be her dad's." Catty pulled on the shades she had borrowed from Serena. "Cool, isn't it?"

They started down the walk together.

"You take shotgun," Catty whispered to Jimena.

"Don't you want to ride in front?" Jimena said, surprised.

"I've seen her drive," Catty warned.

"And?" Jimena asked.

"Just in case." Catty shrugged. "You can grab the steering wheel. You'll know what to do."

"Great." Serena put on her new rimless sunglasses. "Maybe we should have taken the bus."

Payasa snickered. "Jimena can handle anything."

They climbed in and settled into the sun-warmed seats.

"Ready?" Vanessa slipped on oversize sunglasses and a bucket cap, then her lips tightened, and she fumbled with the key. She turned the ignition and after three tries the car thundered to life. She smiled in triumph, then jerked the steering wheel and the car shuddered away from the curb and almost stalled.

Jimena looked at Vanessa. "You're supposed to keep your foot on the accelerator."

"I know that," Vanessa snapped. "But I didn't want to go too fast."

She started again and pulled into the street smoothly this time. At the corner, she made a tight right turn. The front tire rode up over the curb, then bounced down.

Vanessa lowered her glasses and glared at Jimena as if daring her to make a comment. When she didn't, Vanessa pushed her shades back in place, and they sped into traffic.

The sun felt warm on Jimena's face, she started to close her eyes, but then the light ahead turned yellow, and instead of slowing, Vanessa floored the accelerator. She buzzed through the intersection, surprised and a little unsure.

"I love to drive," Vanessa said. "It's the greatest feeling."

At the next crossroads, she signaled to turn left.

She eased forward and tapped her fingers on the steering wheel, waiting for a pause in the oncoming traffic.

The light turned red but two more cars raced through. Immediately, the cross traffic started to claim the intersection. Horns blared.

"I missed the light!" Vanessa started to panic.

"Turn!" Jimena yelled. "You're blocking the intersection."

The car didn't move.

Jimena glanced over. Vanessa's fingers looked like a swarm of gnats gathered around the steering wheel.

"I'm going invisible!" she screamed. In times of extreme emotion, Vanessa had trouble controlling her power.

Catty started laughing, then Payasa joined in.

Jimena grabbed the steering wheel, scattering

Vanessa's molecules. "Take your foot off the brake and push on the gas."

"I can't," Vanessa said, alarmed.

Her foot was gone.

"Sometimes I can move things when I'm invisible but—" Her voice broke and her sunglasses fell from what had once been her face and hit the seat.

Jimena slammed her foot on the gas pedal, gunning the engine. The car turned right, tires screeching, and nearly plowed into a slow-moving Ford that was trying to ease by them. They swerved, then shot in a straight line down the street, and whipped around the first corner in a sharp right turn.

Finally, Jimena steered the car into an empty driveway. She was laughing so hard, her foot slipped off the brake. The car almost plunged into the garage door at the end of the drive. That only made them laugh louder, and this time Vanessa joined in, her voice sounding like the wild cackle of some unseen bird.

A few minutes later, a rematerialized Vanessa

parked the car in front of a large Tudor home in Hancock Park, where Tianna lived.

"How are you doing?" Jimena asked as she opened the car door.

"I think I can handle anything now." Vanessa smiled back at her.

They stepped up a short flight of stairs and followed a brick path to the porch.

Jimena rang the doorbell.

Mary, Tianna's foster mother, answered the door. "Hi, girls." Mary smiled. The house smelled of cookies and furniture polish. "Tianna's not home right now. She's skateboarding."

"Did she tell you where?" Catty asked. "It's kind of important that we find her."

Mary shrugged. "She went off with Derek early. They said that afterward they were going to One Seven."

"If you see her, will you tell her we came by?" Jimena asked.

"Certainly," Mary answered. "You girls have a nice day."

They turned and walked back to the street,

but as Jimena started to get into the car, she saw a flash of blue under one of the bushes at the side of the yard. "That looks like a skateboard."

Catty walked over and pulled it out. "It's Tianna's. I painted the moonscape on the deck."

"Why would she hide it?" Serena asked.

Vanessa shrugged, her fingers running over the helmet and elbow pads tucked under the bush next to the board. "I guess she lied to Mary about what she was doing."

"Or something happened to her," Payasa said.

"What should we do?" Serena looked to Jimena.

"We need to find the Scroll," Jimena said. "Let's go over to UCLA, then after we can catch up with Tianna and Derek at One Seven."

"If they're there," Catty put in.

Jimena nodded, hoping nothing had happened to Tianna.

CHAPTER SIXTEEN

WITHOUT KNOCKING, Catty opened the door to the office at the end of the hallway.

Her mother looked up, startled, and a blush rose to her cheeks. A man was leaning over her, looking at the illuminated manuscript on the desk in front of her, but Jimena had the impression that he had been touching Kendra's hair.

The man stood stiffly and straightened his gray tie, his lips stretching into an unconvincing smile.

"Did we interrupt something?" Catty teased

as they trundled into the small room.

"No," Kendra answered too quickly, her fingers nervously working the purple beads hanging around her neck. She turned to the man. "This is my daughter, Catty, and her friends," she said, touching the man's sleeve with the tips of her fingers. "Girls, meet Professor Hendrix."

Professor Hendrix tipped his head with an arrogant nod and stared at Jimena. "What brings you to campus?"

"Just checking out the school." Vanessa stepped over to a pile of manuscripts laid out on a table.

Jimena studied Professor Hendrix, not sure why she felt such a surge of dislike for him. He was meticulously groomed. His brown hair looked like it had a hundred-dollar cut from one of the upscale salons in Beverly Hills.

"Do you girls have an interest in the classics?" He smoothed his hand down the front of his rich suit as if he were pressing it.

"I do," Payasa answered.

He picked up a pencil and, holding it by

the eraser, used it as a pointer, tapping books at random as he spoke. "We have a world-renowned program here. I'm extremely proud of it. We translate old manuscripts and see how the information can apply to modern science. As an example . . ."

Anxiety stirred inside Jimena, but she wasn't sure why. She only knew she wanted to get out of the room and back into sunshine. She joined Catty and Serena poking around in the stacks behind Kendra's desk.

"Did you finish your mind scan?" Jimena asked Serena.

She nodded.

"What did you get?" Catty asked.

"Your mom doesn't have the Scroll, and neither does Professor Hendrix," Serena answered. "Are you sure you didn't hide it in another part of the house and just forgot? You said yourself you were rattled."

Catty shrugged. "I can look again."

"Let's blow this place." Jimena started walking to the door.

Serena raced ahead of her and curled her hand around the doorknob. "We have to be going."

Jimena squeezed out behind her.

"Yeah," Catty added and stepped into the hallway after her. "Nice to meet you, Professor Hendrix."

Payasa and Vanessa ran after them, their footsteps echoing down the long corridor.

Jimena kept glancing back at the door, not understanding her apprehension. "I don't like him," she said at last, his effect on her still lingering like a dark cloud.

"He's so stuck on himself. Nobody does." Catty sighed heavily. "Except my mom. It's pretty obvious, huh? Can you imagine him as a step-dad?"

Vanessa started to say something, but Jimena interrupted her. "Do you hear sirens?" she asked in disbelief.

"*Ya lo creo.*" Payasa nodded. "I think so."

They hurried to the other end of the hall-way and stared out at the campus through a window. A campus police car pulled up to the building, followed quickly by an LAPD squad car.

"How are they finding you?" Catty asked, her eyes wide with a sense of wonder and fear.

"I think the Atrox is sending them," Jimena answered, again feeling as if she were the object of some dreadful game.

Serena nodded. "There's no other way they could know."

"At least it's not the nymphs this time," Payasa put in.

"I'll take care of it." Vanessa grabbed Jimena's hand.

At once a strange flutter spread through Jimena's body and her heart began to pound. Her skin tingled as it stretched out taut. She held her free hand in front of her, amazed at the way the flesh stirred and pulled apart until it was no more than a hazy foam of small dots.

Her body continued to lengthen, and then at last she was lighter than air and floating up to the ceiling.

The policemen walked under them in slow sure steps, their heads moving from side to side.

Jimena sensed Vanessa's nervousness and could feel her molecules pulling back together. The increased heaviness made them drop three inches. Jimena knew they were becoming visible. She glanced where she thought her leg should be. It looked like a funnel of dust rolling near the fluorescent lights.

Behind her, Vanessa's face was forming. Her panicked expression gave her a ghostlike look. Then with renewed energy she quickened their flow, and they became invisible again, safely heading for the stairwell.

Without warning, the class bell rang even though it was Saturday. The sound buzzed through them, jogging their cells back together. At the top of the stairs, their molecules slammed painfully into place, making them materialize. They fell from the air and tumbled down the steps to the landing.

Jimena felt dazed.

"Sorry." Vanessa sat up, rubbing her elbow. "The noise just startled me too much."

"Come on." Serena thundered down the steps and joined them. "You got past the police. Let's get out of here."

Jimena ran with her friends, kneading the small of her back against the pain. She was grateful to be outside in the sunshine again, but with a shock she realized the sun was easing toward the horizon. Another day had almost passed and she still didn't know how to change the future.

Back in the car, Vanessa turned and faced them. "Maybe we should visit Maggie and see if she knows a way to find the Scroll. We could also ask her about Jimena's premonition."

"She won't be back until Sunday night." Serena settled into the backseat and put on her shades. "She said she had some important ceremony to prepare for."

"What ceremony?" Vanessa asked. "She didn't mention anything to me."

"I don't know." Serena shrugged. "I mean, she does have a life that doesn't involve us."

"Let's get our mind off the Scroll," Catty pleaded. "I don't want to think about it for a while at least."

"We need to get ready to go over to One Seven," Jimena said. "And meet Tianna."

"I hope she shows up." Vanessa started the car.

"She will," Catty answered, and then a mischievous grin covered her face and she tapped Vanessa's shoulder. "Do you think we could raid your mom's storage room?"

"Vanessa's mom works as a costume designer for the movies," Serena explained to Payasa. "She uses their third bedroom to store the clothes she's designed. It's incredible."

Vanessa opened the door to her mother's storage room and switched on a light. The smells of rose sachet and mothballs drifted around them as they walked inside.

Payasa whistled. "It's like a store."

"Only the price is right." Catty started looking through the waves and waves of dresses hanging on racks, arranged by color, style, and length.

Payasa searched through the green dresses, humming merrily. She pulled out a mini and posed in front of a large mirror in the corner, then turned showing it off. "Your mom did this?"

Vanessa nodded and stepped into low-rise gold slacks. "Yeah, sometimes the outfits she designs are really cool—but other times—boy, are they weird."

"You're lucky," Payasa said, trying on the dress. "Everything my mother sews for me has ribbons and lace, like I'm still her little baby girl."

"Mom got some false eyelashes from the makeup department," Vanessa added. "Not the fake kind, but the real feathery ones like the stars wear. I'm going to try them tonight."

"Me, too!" Catty slipped into a soft fuchsia tube top and pulled on matching sleeves. "And I want to try some of those body-art stickers she was showing us."

Serena put on a strapless lace top with black beaded fringe over hip-hugging slacks, then she used stencils to draw three red stars on her cheeks. "Check it out."

Jimena took a silky top and pretended to look at herself in the mirror, but she was surreptitiously studying her friends. They didn't seem to be hiding anything from her, and yet she knew one of them was. She began to shudder.

"Jimena?" Serena stared at her.

Jimena tried to pull her lips into a reassuring smile, but when she glanced at her reflection, she was startled by how distressed she looked.

"Are you all right?" Serena stepped next to her.

"Everything's fine," she lied. "I'm just having a hard time deciding."

"I'll decide for you then." Serena handed her a blue skirt and halter top.

Jimena stared at it, knowing it was something Collin would pick out. Reluctantly, she changed into the silky outfit, then followed her friends back outside to the car.

By the time they took the escalators up from the underground parking structure into the new shopping center on Hollywood and Highland, the sun had set. Full dark closed around them, and with growing desperation, Jimena realized she now had less that twenty-four hours to act.

"Look at those *vatos* checking us out." A sultry smile crossed Payasa's lips. She wore eyeliner stickers over her top lashes and a pearly powder over her body.

Jimena knew they looked good, and normally she would have joined in the fun, but tonight her stomach clenched with anxiety. She had only one thing on her mind. She needed to find out which one of her friends was the traitor, and quickly. A hopeless feeling overwhelmed her. Even if she did know, she still had no idea how she was going to change the future.

They got off the escalators and started walking to the club. Catty stopped abruptly, and Jimena bumped into her.

"We have to show ID to go inside." Catty pointed to the sign.

"What are we going to do now?" Jimena asked. "I don't have anything I can show."

"Man, they want a twenty-dollar cover charge." Payasa sounded rankled. "Why does everything cost so much on this side of town?"

Jimena, Catty, and Vanessa turned and looked at Serena.

"What?" she asked.

"Do your stuff." Catty nudged her. "Throw in a little mind fix so we can go inside."

"We're not supposed to use our powers that way," Serena said firmly.

"Just do it," Jimena coaxed. "It's the only way to get inside and find Tianna."

"I can't do that," Serena answered. "It's wrong."

"I can," a deep pleasant voice said. Stanton stepped from behind Serena and kissed her cheek.

Vanessa looked at Jimena. "It's the only way." She shrugged, and started after Stanton and Serena.

"Come on," Jimena said to Payasa.

They walked to the front of the line where a guy stood with his pockets turned out for a security guard. Stanton said something to a bald man with multiple chins. The man smiled and shook hands with Stanton as if he had known him for a long time, then he opened the door and waved them through.

"What did he do?" Payasa asked as they walked past the grinning man.

"He used mind control," Jimena explained. "And made the guy think we'd already showed ID and paid."

The kids still waiting in line for a weapons check stared enviously.

Inside, the lights were dim and the music strong. Jimena scanned the crowd. "I don't see Tianna."

"Let's spread out," Vanessa suggested. "This place is huge." She crossed her fingers. "I hope Michael gets to perform here soon. I want to sing on that stage."

"Meet back at the entrance." Catty waved and hurried off.

Vanessa and Payasa started toward the DJ booth.

Jimena stopped at the edge of the dance

floor and watched Serena and Stanton. She wondered if Serena's love for Stanton could have convinced her to change sides. The Daughters had freed Stanton from the Atrox once, but afterward he had become a Follower again. He had claimed it was the only way he could have saved Serena from Lambert, a powerful member of the Inner Circle. But now he was Prince of Night, and even though he had rescued Serena a second time, Jimena didn't trust him. She sensed there was something more going on between them, especially now that Serena wore Hekate's orb along with her moon amulet.

Stanton glanced at Jimena as if he had read her thoughts, and still looking at her he tenderly cupped Serena's face and kissed her.

Jimena scowled and started to walk away when someone tapped her shoulder. Collin stood behind her. He looked incredible in his black sweater and tight jeans. She felt flustered and didn't know what to do. She hadn't expected to see him here.

"Want to dance?" he asked.

She hesitated. She couldn't pull her mind away from the image of him naked.

"I'm sorry about last night," she stammered and blushed.

"It's all right." He smiled as if he knew what she was envisioning. That only made her blush deepen.

"Dance with me?"

She nodded and put her hands on his chest. He took the tips of her fingers and wrapped her hands around his neck, then he clasped his around her waist. His touch sent a quiver of delight through her.

She closed her eyes and rested her cheek tentatively against his. She breathed in the scent of his aftershave, wishing she could stay in his arms the entire evening. Her chest ached from missing him so badly.

His breath tickled the back of her neck, sending a sweet chill up her spine, then his lips moved against her hair. "Surf was great today." His words felt like soft kisses against her ear.

"I wish I had been there," she said, and immediately wished she had chosen other words. Had she sounded too desperate?

She glanced to the side.

Tianna had entered the club with Derek.

"Let's go say hi to Tianna." Jimena pulled away from Collin. She didn't bother to look back to see if he was following her.

Normally, Tianna looked like a goddess, but tonight her black hair lacked luster and fell flat against her face as if she had been sweating. Her eyes looked red, swollen, and tired. She held a wad of tissues in one hand.

"Hey, Jimena." Tianna coughed hoarsely and wiped her nose.

Derek shook his head. "I told her to stay home in bed, but she wanted to check out the club."

"We missed you today," Jimena declared. "Mary said you went skateboarding, but then we saw your board and pads hidden under the bushes. So I guess you had something else planned?"

"Mary doesn't understand that sometimes I just want to hang out, so I lied to her." Tianna sniffed, her eyes watering. "I spent the day with Derek." She glanced up at him as if waiting for him to agree.

"Yeah, we spent the day together." Derek stammered, turning his eyes away.

"Doing what?" Jimena asked, knowing they were hiding something,.

"You're just like Mary," Tianna snapped. "We were just hanging out."

Jimena eased away from them. Time was running out, and she didn't even know which one of her friends would betray the others tomorrow night. Her anxiety began to build. She sensed that the only person she could trust right now was her sworn enemy Payasa. She searched through the dance floor until she found her.

"What's up?" Payasa asked as they started walking toward the exit.

"I need a safe place to stay for the night," Jimena confided.

"I've got you covered," Payasa said as they hurried outside to Hollywood Boulevard.

They walked six blocks before they turned

and headed south through a residential neighborhood of small stucco homes. Tree branches formed a canopy overhead, blotting out the light from the street lamps. They had only gone a short distance when they heard someone walking behind them.

They slipped into the shadows and waited, nerves tingling and hot. Jimena held her breath, knowing Payasa was doing the same, and listened for a sound to give the person away.

Furtive footsteps trod down the walk, coming toward them. A moment later, a hand touched Jimena's shoulder.

▼

CHAPTER SEVENTEEN

J

IMENA SPUN AROUND.

Chris stood behind her, dressed in a muscle-T and jeans, looking like a regular high-school guy. "Is he another one?" Payasa asked.

"Kinda," Jimena answered.

"I'm sorry I had to leave you so abruptly in the forest." Chris glanced down the silent street. "I came back for you, but you were gone."

"I hitched," Jimena said. "Are the nymphs after you, too?"

"No." He stepped into darker shadows. "But I must warn you about Gerard de Molaire."

The words sent a shudder through Jimena and she wondered why she should have such a physical reaction to someone's name. "Who's that?"

"A powerful sorcerer," Chris explained. "He was once a member of the Society of Winged Dragons."

"What?" Payasa asked.

"Alchemist and sorcerers who made pacts with the Atrox. In exchange for their allegiance, the Atrox gave them spirits to help them perform their arcane magic. Gerard requested the three nymphs formed from the blood of the Gorgon Medusa. He has controlled them ever since."

"But why is he sending the nymphs after me?" Jimena rested her head against a tree.

"Back in the thirteenth century when I had first been assigned to be Keeper of the Scroll—"

Payasa looked like the breath had just gotten knocked out of her. Jimena clasped her hand to steady her.

Chris continued, "Gerard placed his seal on the Scroll. He told me that he had done it to help me. If the seal were ever broken, then I would know that someone had used the Scroll. But I never trusted him as the others did. I sensed that Gerard had sealed the Scroll because he didn't want me to see what he had hidden inside."

"Did you break his seal?" Jimena asked.

Chris shook his head. "I tricked him. I slipped a long, red-hot needle under his seal close to the parchment and melted the wax, so I was able to lift his seal without breaking any of it, and later I set it back."

"What did you find?" Payasa asked.

"I discovered that Gerard had hidden a spell within the Scroll."

"But why would he do that?" Jimena wondered.

"Because only the heir to the Scroll can destroy it, and he knew that if he inscribed his spell within the Scroll, it would remain safely hidden until the twenty-first century. The Scroll's curse would not only protect the Scroll, but also his incantation, until he could use it to create a new future."

"One where the Atrox reigns," Jimena said, feeling defeated already.

Chris shook his head. "His spell changes the future and makes him the one in control."

"So why didn't he do it before?" Payasa asked. "I mean, he waited so many centuries."

"He needed the right alignment of the stars for his magic to work," Chris explained.

"Why didn't you try to stop him after you discovered what he had done?" Jimena glanced nervously at the shadows swimming across the yard behind them.

"I did. I showed my discovery to the others, but they laughed at my suspicions and called Gerard's magic harmless."

"Do you know when he's going to do this?" Jimena asked, already sensing that she had the answer.

"My astrological calculations suggested that the catastrophe would occur in the beginning of the twenty-first century on the night the constellation of the Seven Sisters and the full moon were directly overhead at midnight. Such an alignment has always been foreseen as marking the end of the world."

"Sunday night," Jimena whispered with a shudder.

Chris nodded. "Gerard needs to channel the energy of the Atrox in order to alter the future into the one he desires. But in order to avoid the curse of the Scroll, he must deceive someone else into using the Scroll to summon the Atrox."

"A Daughter?" Jimena wondered if this could be the traitor she had seen in her premonition.

Chris nodded.

"Do you know who?" Jimena asked.

He shook his head. "You must find out and stop him," Chris continued. "In this new future, the forces of good have been stripped of all power."

Jimena stared at him. "Can you tell me how?" Her voice sounded desperate.

"I don't have the answer," he whispered. "If I

did, I would have acted already, but it is your destiny to do this."

The words chilled her.

She closed her eyes. "I'm afraid I'm going to fail."

When she opened them again, Chris was gone, and Payasa was staring at her.

For a few moments, they stood there in silence.

"Come on," Payasa said finally. "I know a safe place to spend the night."

CHAPTER EIGHTEEN

GRAFFITI SPRAY-PAINTED over billboards, garages, fences, and homes claimed the neighborhood as Wilshire 5 territory. Jimena kept her face in shadows now. Her nerves thrummed alert to the danger of being in this part of town. She was from El Nueve, and not welcome here.

In the distance she could hear the beat of gangster rap and knew the Saturday night party had begun.

"This is where I kick it with my homies."

Payasa motioned with her head when they turned the corner.

Jimena had seen the garage a dozen times before, mostly from the window of a speeding car. Inside a yellow lightbulb dangled at the end of an extension cord thrown over a crossbeam. It swung back and forth, making shadows swirl, and gave an odd orange glow to the faces of the kids sitting on folding chairs. In the driveway, couples danced and took turns drinking from bottles wrapped in brown paper bags.

"You'd better let me talk to them first," Payasa warned.

Jimena nodded and stepped back against a tree. She didn't think it was going to be as easy as that. It had been a while since she had gone on a mission against Wilshire 5, but gangs had long memories.

"I don't think this will work." Jimena surveyed the guys her age and younger, leaning against a wire fence. They held cigarettes in one hand and choked the necks of beer bottles in the other, their eyes fixed on the girls dancing at the party. They spoke in low voices, making plans for their next ride. The older ones had already left the hood and were ballers now. She had seen them down at Planet Bang and in shopping malls; the Tommy boys blending in at fancy restaurants, but still living the gangster life.

"What do you want to do, then?" Payasa asked.

A guy wearing baggy khakis and a white T-shirt turned and started walking toward them, his hand resting on his waistband. Jimena tensed, ready to run, and for the first time it occurred to her that Payasa could be setting her up.

"Chill," Payasa warned. "It's Tavio."

Tavio had a bad reputation. Even kids in Ninth Street admired him. There was no way Jimena could outrun him and a gun.

"*Oye*, Payasa, you look good." Tavio didn't have the shaved head of the other guys. A hair net protected his perfect combed-back style. Tattoos on his arms and neck declared his allegiance to Wilshire 5. A wound on the side of his face looked like the result of a recent fight.

He stopped when he saw Jimena and she knew he was reaching under his T-shirt to rest his fingers on the cold heavy metal of a gun.

"*De dónde?*" he whispered, as if he enjoyed hitting her up. She was a *leyenda*, and his eyes said he wanted to be the one to bring the legend down.

She fought the desire to lift her head up and answer, *Nueve. ¿Y qué?* What are you going to do about it? She couldn't tonight, and not answering made her stomach burn.

For a moment they stared at each other, and Jimena knew he could see the *peligro* in her eyes. Maybe knowing she was going to die put a darker danger in her gaze. She curled her lips and watched him frown.

"It's okay." Payasa nudged him. "She's with me."

He eyed Jimena, considering. When she didn't do more, he touched the lump on the side of his head as if it were still tender. "I heard you got busted for that *cabron* over in Lincoln Heights."

"What did you hear?" she asked, her heart settling down.

"This *vato* was bragging how he hired three *linda*-looking girls to do some selling for him. They got busted right away, but they didn't rat him out. He said they fingered you, and you got locked up for something he did."

Jimena looked at Payasa, then back at Tavio. "How do you know so much?"

"I used to do some deals with him." Tavio smiled menacingly. He took a Polaroid photo from his back pocket. It was creased as if he had pulled it out a hundred times to look at it. He glanced around suddenly cautious, not wanting anyone else to see, and handed it to Jimena.

"As soon as he hooked up with those three girls he started treating me like I was his *bracero*." Tavio had hate in his eyes. "I went over to his house, and he hit me with the bat and took my picture with a Polaroid. Then he threw the photo at me like I was one of his *tecatos* begging drugs in the middle of the night. He says, 'This is what you get when you come by too late and wake me up.'"

Jimena stared down at the picture. The image

was blurred, but she could still make out the bat against Tavio's head.

"Why didn't you hit back?" Jimena asked suspiciously. The insult was too close to the bone; Tavio should have retaliated already.

"I don't want to get even. I want to ruin him, take all his stuff, but he doesn't keep it in the house, so it wasn't there for me to steal." A wicked smile crept over his face and he pulled a key from his side pocket. "Stupid *gabacho* didn't ask for his key back." He handed it to Jimena. "You need to take him down more than I do."

She wrapped her hand around the key. She wanted to get the guy, but not just for herself. She needed to clear her name so her grandmother and brother wouldn't think she had fallen back into her old bad ways. "Do you know where he keeps the stuff?"

Tavio looked back at the slow-moving girls dancing in the garage and spoke softly. "The stash has to be close to his house, because he never leaves for more than three minutes when he goes to get it, but I don't think he keeps it in his yard. If the cops found it there, they could confiscate his house, car, and money."

Jimena's heart found a faster beat, anticipating the danger. She liked the feel of adrenaline rushing through her body. Already her mind was racing, trying to find a plan.

"He's got some bad stuff now," Tavio went on. "Sixteen kids took a ride to the hospital on his *drogas*."

Jimena wondered if that was why the cops were so desperate to catch her; they thought it was her fault. "I got a plan," she said finally.

A few minutes later, Jimena and Payasa had changed into black sweats and were speeding down the Pasadena Freeway with Tavio. East of the L.A. riverbed, they took an off-ramp and entered Lincoln Heights. Tavio turned off the headlights, and they rolled silently through rows of small storefront businesses and used-car lots, then into a residential area. They parked at a corner under the streetlight.

"That house at the end with the old Ford

parked in the drive," Tavio said. "The key goes to the back door."

"Call the police in one hour." Jimena started to climb out.

"What if you're not back?" he asked.

Something in her face must have convinced him. He glanced down at the green digital read-out on the display panel.

"One hour," he agreed. "Don't wimp out."

"Chale." Payasa brushed him off and shut the car door.

Jimena and Payasa walked down the side-walk, their Nikes beating a fast rhythm on the crumbling concrete walk and soon they were near the house. As one, they dodged into the driveway, ducked behind the scuffed fender of the old Ford, then took careful steps to the back of the house where a black Corvette was parked under a carport.

The lawn was a rich thick carpet and smelled as if it had just been cut. A concrete block wall fenced the yard on two sides, but on the third a line of orange trees, heavy with fruit, made a barrier.

"No place to hide anything here," Payasa whispered.

Jimena nodded in agreement, and got down on her hands and knees. She crawled around the base of the house, checking the screens over the openings to the crawl spaces. All had been nailed shut.

As she started to stand she caught a glimpse of a glossy trail across the lawn to the orange trees. From her angle it looked as if someone had stepped across the yard several times that night, their footsteps bending down the newly cut grass.

She stood and hurried silently to the trees, then bent beneath the branches. The tangy citrus smell filled her lungs.

"What did you find?" Payasa asked, brushing leaves aside. An orange fell to the ground with a light thump.

"Over there." Jimena stomped through a path that had been made in knee-high weeds.

In the back of the neighboring yard, an old rusted Dodge, tires removed, rested on cinder blocks. The bumper was dented and the windshield cracked.

Jimena stepped around to the trunk. The key lock looked new, its metal shining in the moonlight. She looked at Payasa and smiled.

"Now all we have to do is find the key to the trunk." Payasa tapped her watch. "Fifteen minutes have gone by."

"He'll have the keys with him," Jimena said.

Back at the house, Jimena pressed her ear against the door and listened. When she heard nothing, she turned the key, carefully wrapped her hand around the doorknob, and pulled it open. She flinched at the sudden creaking sound.

When she stepped onto the back porch and into the kitchen, she felt as if hot wires were running through her legs. Her mouth went dry, and she licked her lips.

Payasa followed, clinging to the shadows inside, her breathing heavy now.

A clock ticked on the wall and a refrigerator hummed. They crept into the living room. Jimena stopped and put her hand on Payasa's arm to caution her. Near the door, a tall guy with long hair and defined muscles lay sleeping on a beanbag chair, a baseball bat across his lap.

Payasa pointed to a set of keys on the coffee table. She crept over to it and picked it up, then quietly they eased back outside and ran across the lawn to the neighboring yard.

Jimena tried the keys in the lock. Finally one slipped in, and the trunk popped open. Disappointment flowed through her. The inside was jammed with dozens of trash bags filled with worn clothing.

In frustration, she slammed her hand into the bags. A small rattling sound gave her hope. She turned and looked at Payasa. "Pills?" She pulled a pink sweater from the bag. Underneath were bundles of plastic-wrapped white pills.

Payasa picked a pair of jeans from the top of the next bag, and beneath it were stacks of red, blue, and green balloons, deflated with the ends tied to keep the contents inside. Jimena knew in an instant that the man was dealing more than Ecstasy. She felt disgusted, wondering if he had ever sold to her mother.

She picked up a bag, heaved it over her shoulder, and waited for Payasa to do the same.

"Do you think this is the stuff sending the kids to the hospital?" Payasa asked as they bent under the tree branches. Oranges rained down on them with soft thumping sounds.

"Maybe," Jimena answered as they headed back to the house.

They waited on the porch until they heard the man's gruff snore, then they eased into the living room, set the bags down, and stacked the plastic bundles on the scratched coffee table.

When they were finished, they hurried back outside.

"Go to Tavio," Jimena ordered. "I'll get what's left and take it inside."

Payasa didn't move. "I'll wait for you."

Jimena stared at her. "If the cops catch me again what will it matter?"

Payasa chewed the side of her mouth, then turned and hurried away.

Jimena went back to the old Dodge and

lugged two more bags back to the house. She paused listening for sound, then cautiously crept through the kitchen and into the living room. She set the bags down, opened the first, started removing its contents and froze.

The beanbag chair was empty.

Panic seized her. Her breathing was coming in rapid gasps. Where was he?

Then she heard a toilet flush. As soon as he came back to the room he would see the plastic bundles in the light cast from the street lamp outside.

Footsteps filled the small house. She looked frantically around for a place to hide. She would be seen anywhere in the living room if he turned on the lamp.

Her legs trembled as she stepped over the trash bags and hurried back to the kitchen. She hesitated between the two rooms, wondering if she should dart out the back door.

Without warning the refrigerator opened, and she saw the man's silhouette. He leaned inside, still holding his baseball bat. The metal spikes on his wrist cuff shot shards of light across the room as he pulled out a beer.

Jimena pressed back against the wall and waited, totally exposed. He must have used a bathroom that she hadn't seen on the back porch.

She needed to find a place to hide, but she was afraid that if she moved now he would see her in the corner of his eye.

The man balanced the bat in the crook of his arm and grabbed a bag of potato chips from the top of the refrigerator. He kicked the door closed, and she used the noise and change of light as a cover and scurried under the table.

Her heart beat so fiercely she was certain he could hear it. She opened her mouth and breathed slowly, her lungs ready to explode.

He started back to the living room, his heavy boots inches from her fingers as he stepped across the linoleum. What would he do when he saw the drugs they had left on the coffee table?

In the distance she thought she heard sirens, but she wasn't sure. Blood roared through her head.

The man turned to go into the living room with slow easy steps. She glanced back at the outside door, measuring her chances of outrunning him. She could, if he didn't have the baseball bat in his hand.

She bit her lip and started to stand, but the back door opened. Her breath caught, and she dove under the table again as an overweight guy walked boldly into the house, stripping off a windbreaker. His steps were so heavy she could feel the vibrations in the floor under her palms.

She definitely heard sirens now. Then the lights went on in the living room and a loud crashing sound followed as if the tall guy had swung his bat against the wall in frustration. He continued cursing. The large guy joined him, their angry voices rising.

Jimena's instinct clicked in and took over. The sirens were close now, and the dealers were going to have to choose between chasing her and hiding their stuff.

She eased up and stood, then sprinted across the kitchen to the door.

The guys started after her, the tall one swinging his bat, but as she leaped from the porch, a police car pulled up in front. The bar lights flashed jaggedly over the yard. The guys stopped chasing her and ran back to the house.

Jimena scrambled up and over the gray concrete block wall.

Payasa was waiting for her on the other side. "Come on."

They ran down the street, their feet slapping across the pavement, and dove into the car as Tavio jammed the gear into drive. He slammed his foot on the accelerator, and they jarred forward, blasting into the night.

CHAPTER NINETEEN

JIMENA DREAMED THAT Collin was kissing her, only his lips felt like Jell-O being smeared over her face in broad strokes. She woke up with a start, but the slimy feeling didn't go away. Then she smelled the doggy breath and opened her eyes.

"Wolf!"

He pressed his cold nose into her cheek, and his large tongue lashed across her lips. She sunk her fingers into the thick fur behind his ears and tried to hold him back, but he jumped up and set his paws on her chest.

Payasa sat on the bed, laughing. "He came home this morning all muddy with four streaks of dried blood in his fur. Didn't you, boy?"

Wolf whined deep in his throat, then exploded into barks and pranced, wagging his tail.

Payasa waved a white envelope in front of Jimena. "I got the tickets for the concert. And after I told my homies what you did, they chipped in and rented a limo for us."

"A limo?" Jimena swung her legs over the side of Payasa's bed.

"A stretch like the movie stars use," Payasa answered. She was already dressed in bagged-out jeans, Pendleton, and heavy work shoes. "If it's going to be our last ride, we might as well make it a good one. The limo's waiting for us."

"Already?"

"You slept the day away." Payasa walked over to the dresser, picked up a worn pair of jeans and a blue Pendleton, and carried them back to Jimena. "Get dressed."

Minutes later, they were seated in the back of a long, sleek black limousine. Payasa swiveled the

TV toward them and pulled a can of Pepsi from the ice bin.

Jimena bent over and, crouching low, made her way to the seat behind the driver. She slid the glass partition open. "Could you stop at my grandmother's apartment first?"

"Sure." The driver smiled and wrote down the address on a white pad clipped on the dashboard.

Jimena crept back to her seat and stared out the tinted windows. Blue and orange neon lights blurred over couples strolling with their children. Crowds gathered outside music stores, gyms, and coffee shops. Even bangers had deserted their thug mentality to walk the streets and feel the joy of perfect weather and a full moon rising.

"Why are we stopping at your grand-mother's?" Payasa asked.

"I need ID." Jimena looked at Payasa. "So they can identify my body. I don't want my grand-mother wondering what happened to me for the rest of her life."

Payasa nodded knowingly and picked her student ID from her shirt pocket.

In a few blocks the limousine pulled up to the curb. The driver got out and opened the door for Jimena. Heads turned and people stared, hoping to see a celebrity. She could sense their disappointment when they didn't recognize her face.

She hurried toward the brick apartment building that had been converted from an old hotel. She didn't have the key but buzzed the manager on the intercom.

"Hello," Mrs. Zuckerman answered in a cheerful voice.

"It's Jimena. I got locked out."

"I'll leave the extra key in your door. Don't forget to return it, eh?"

The magnetic lock buzzed and Jimena stepped inside.

She headed past the sweeping stairs of the old hotel that had led up to a ballroom and went to the elevator.

Mrs. Zuckerman had left the key in the keyhole. Jimena unlocked the door and slipped into the dark living room.

Her grandmother was in the kitchen, kneeling in front of her altar, a small table filled with flowers and pictures of saints. She held a rosary in both hands, her fingers pinching a bead as her lips moved in prayer. Light from the candle flames flickered across her aged face. A lump of pom incense on a small prayer board glowed yellow, lighting the serene statue of La Morena. The bitter smoke seeped into the air.

Jimena moved stealthily to her grandmother's bedroom, then lifted the top of an old trunk and breathed in the camphor smell of mothballs. She rummaged through her baby clothes, found a worn manila envelope, and pulled out her birth certificate, then got up, folded the paper, slipped it into her back pocket, and hurried toward the door.

She started across the living room when something made her turn back. Her grandmother stood at the kitchen sink, staring out a small window at the night sky. A huge silvery moon rose between two buildings.

Sadness overwhelmed Jimena. Her grandmother had told her that people die three times. First, when they physically die, second, when they're put in the ground never to be seen on earth again, and third, when no one remains alive with their memories. Jimena had always thought that she would outlive her grandmother, but now it was going to be the other way around. She wondered what memories her grandmother would cherish, and at the same time her chest ached with regret. She wished she could go back and change the bad things she had done.

Her grandmother turned suddenly.

"*M'ija?*" She walked slowly toward her, the rosary still clutched in her hand. "Not even an hour ago, I talked to you on the telephone. You were just leaving to catch the Greyhound to come back to Los Angeles. How are you here?" Her old eyes looked at Jimena as if she were seeing a miracle.

"I don't have time to tell you everything." Jimena touched her grandmother's frail shoulder, longing for the comfort of her embrace.

"What, *m'ijita?* You're crying." Her grandmother brushed the tears from Jimena's face.

"You know how I can see the future?" She didn't wait for her grandmother to answer. "I had another premonition. This time I saw my own death."

Her grandmother drew in her breath sharply. "Did your angel bring you to me so I could see you one last time before . . . ?"

"*Abuelita*, the angel who came to help you the night I was born, she was *una diosa*, a goddess of the moon."

Her grandmother's hand moved to touch Jimena's amulet, but it was gone. "You're not wearing the necklace she gave you that night. You were never supposed to take it off."

Jimena nodded. "I couldn't help it. *Abuelita*, the reason I can see the future, it's because I'm here to protect people from an ancient evil, and tonight I have to do something dangerous, and I don't think I'll survive."

"Tonight?" her grandmother answered as if her words had special meaning to her.

Jimena nodded.

Her grandmother pulled her to the kitchen

window and pointed to the sky. "Look at the constellation of the Seven Sisters and the way the full moon is rising," her grandmother said in an ominous voice. "According to the Aztec and the Maya, both will be overhead at midnight when the world comes to an end. Tonight this will happen."

A chill raced through Jimena and she glanced at the line of candles behind the incense. "That's why you've been praying so hard."

Her grandmother nodded. "A bad feeling has been with me all day."

"Pray for me also. I'm trying to stop a catastrophe, but I don't know if I can." She paused and looked into her grandmother's eyes. "I'm scared."

"You must be stronger than you have ever imagined you could be." Her grandmother embraced her, holding her tightly.

A heavy despair spread through Jimena. The future was waiting for her, and there was nothing she could do but face it.

CHAPTER TWENTY

"LET ME LOOK AT your birth certificate," Payasa said as soon as Jimena settled into her seat.

Jimena pulled the paper from her back pocket and gave it to Payasa.

The limousine pulled away from the curb, circled the block back to Wilshire, then turned left, heading east toward downtown.

"I thought you and I were the same age?" Payasa asked, a puzzled look on her face.

"We are," Jimena answered.

"But you're going to be seventeen." Payasa handed the birth certificate back to her.

Jimena grabbed it and studied her birth date. It said she had been born a year earlier than she thought. "Why would my grandmother lie to me?"

"She's old." Payasa shrugged. "Maybe she forgot."

"Not my *abuelita*."

Now Jimena had a new concern. Every Daughter had to make an important decision on her seventeenth birthday. She could either choose to lose her powers and her memories of being a goddess, or she could transform into something else, a spirit perhaps. None of them knew what happened to the ones who chose the transformation. The ones who were too frightened to change remained human, but without their powers and with no memory of what they had once been. She shivered, wondering now if she had enough time left to do what was needed.

She glanced down at the birth certificate again. If it was accurate, then she had less than six hours. But she had been born in the desert, her birth registered days later. The information could be wrong. She sighed heavily.

"If it upsets you so much, call your grandmother and ask her why she didn't tell you your real age." Payasa reached for the limo phone but as she handed it to Jimena, the driver pumped the brakes and the car started to slow.

"What the——?" the driver said, surprised.

Jimena looked out the front windshield.

Lizelle stood in the road, her wings spread, blocking the street. Her unearthly beauty was so striking, Jimena had a hard time pulling her eyes away. Azera and Zonda walked toward the rear of the limousine, their dangerous talons scraping the metal sides. Neon lights reflected off their gold scales, sending a flourish of brilliant colors into the night.

"Are they angels?" the limo driver asked, his voice shrouded in disbelief.

"An evil kind," Jimena warned.

Payasa unsnapped her seat belt and opened the car door. Jimena pushed out behind her.

Azera lunged forward. The tips of her claws ripped Jimena's Pendleton.

Jimena and Payasa darted through the crowd that had gathered to watch.

Up and down the sidewalk people stood spellbound, a mixture of fear and awe on their faces. Some took refuge behind cars and inside stores, peering back at the nymphs.

"There!" Jimena pointed to the entrance of an underground parking structure.

They burst into a sprint, their footsteps thundering behind them, and charged down the steep spiraling ramp.

"How did they find us again?" Payasa asked, her words booming into the vast underground lot.

"Something else sent them," Jimena answered. "The same force that sent the cops."

"The Sorcerer?" Payasa asked, breathless.

"Maybe," Jimena answered.

Cars crowded the parking slots. Heat and fumes from engines lingered in the air with an odd metallic scent.

"Here." Jimena yanked Payasa's arm and

pulled her behind an old Cadillac with giant fins.

They lay flat on their stomachs, their cheeks resting against the dirty concrete, the smells of oil and gasoline filling their lungs.

The parking structure became deadly silent.

"You go on," Jimena whispered to Payasa, her lips moving against the cold floor. "There's still time for you to escape. We don't both need to die."

"We could have really been something together if we'd stayed best friends." Payasa's face had a haunted look.

The air stirred, whirling the dust into tiny puffs.

"Go before they get here," Jimena ordered in a low voice.

An eerie cry echoed through the parking structure; Lizelle was communicating with the others, her song coming steadily closer.

"We're dead," Payasa whispered.

"No," Jimena answered. "They only want me. Leave."

"I never planned it this way," Payasa said without moving, her eyes glistening with tears.

"Go!" Jimena urged.

Payasa stared at nothing. "I don't even like the person I've become."

An unnatural breeze fluttered around them, ruffling their hair.

Payasa looked at Jimena. "If those creatures are still trying to stop you from getting to the Staples Center, then whatever you need to change must happen there."

"I know," Jimena answered. "It gives me hope."

Suddenly, Payasa stood.

At first Jimena thought she was going to leave, but instead of running deeper into the parking structure, Payasa let out a fierce cry and ran toward the sound of Lizelle's plaintive voice.

"No!" Jimena screamed.

But before Jimena could run out to stop her, the nymphs swept around Payasa. Their excitement in capturing her electrified their voices. Their eerie singing rose higher than Payasa's screams. They folded their tremendous wings around her, making a tight cocoon, and then they disappeared, taking Payasa with them.

The air grew still again.

Jimena felt heartsick, unable to move. Payasa had sacrificed her life so Jimena could continue. She couldn't let her die in vain. Abruptly, Jimena stood and charged outside, her feet slamming on the pavement. She shoved through the waiting crowd and headed down the street toward the Staples Center, ready to meet her destiny.

CHAPTER TWENTY-ONE

BREATHLESS, JIMENA slowed her steps and joined the crowd walking from the public parking areas toward the Staples Center. The huge gathering was like a musical melting pot. Headbangers, hip-hoppers, punk rockers strolled together, some singing, their energy high and contagious, and seeming to vibrate into the air.

They passed guys selling T-shirts with the band's picture on the front. Other vendors held posters and glow sticks in their hands.

A horn honked in quick beats and then someone called her name. "Jimena!"

She turned.

Collin waved from behind the wheel of his utility van and swung the vehicle to the curb. He looked angry and tired. She stepped to the van as the automatic window rolled down.

"I don't have time—"

"Get in the car." He leaned over and opened the door for her. He had dark circles under his eyes. "I'll give you a ride to the center."

Reluctantly, she climbed in and buckled her seat belt.

"I've been looking for you since last night." He eased into the slow-moving traffic. "You should have told someone where you were going. I was worried something had happened to you. Everyone was."

"Right." She sighed. "If you were so worried, then why did you break up with me?"

"You're the one who always acted like the relationship wasn't important, not me," he answered defensively.

Her head whipped around. "What?"

"Even Friday night. You didn't act happy to see me. You only wanted to talk to Serena."

"You had already found your girlie-girl to replace me!" Jimena's voice was tight with anger, and it hurt her throat to speak. "I saw you with her at Corrine's party."

"Melissa?" The ire dropped from his voice, replaced by surprise.

"I don't know her name." Jimena folded her arms over her chest. "And I don't care."

"You're jealous of Melissa?"

"I'm not *celosa* of anybody."

"Melissa is Hunter's younger sister. She just started going out and she's shy. I was trying to give her some confidence. I don't have any special kind of interest in her." And then the anger returned to his voice with a sudden flash. "Not like your interest in Robert!"

"Robert? I don't like Robert," Jimena shot back.

Collin jerked the steering wheel. The car lunged to the side of the road and jarred to a stop. Horns honked in protest. He set the brake, then grabbed Jimena's hand, pulling her to him. She hadn't anticipated his touch. It sent a shock of adrenaline rushing through her. His fingers curled under her chin and he made her look into his eyes.

She glanced up at him, trying not to give in. His breath caressed her face, his lips inches from hers now.

He smiled and looked down at her. "I'm not interested in her. I'm in love with you."

Her lower lip trembled and she tried to push back tears. "I was going to tell you how I felt at the sleepover tonight, but you broke up with me."

"Tell me."

"I think I'm falling in love with you." The words were out and she felt as if she were going to faint. "I hold my emotions back because I'm afraid of getting hurt. I can take the physical pain, but not the heartbreak kind."

His hand brushed over her cheek and he kissed her lightly.

"I'm sorry," she whispered.

"I never wanted to break up with you," he said. "But you were acting so tough. I thought you didn't care. Then when we did break up, it seemed like that was what you wanted."

Abruptly, she pulled away from him and wiped the tears from her cheeks. "It's too late now." She opened the car door.

He looked surprised. "Where are you going?"

She bailed out. "There's no time left," she yelled over her shoulder and started pushing wildly through the crowd. She had to get to the Staples Center. She didn't even know yet who the traitor was, and she had to stop that Daughter from summoning the Atrox.

Moments later, she paused under the purple glow of lights, not sure where she should go. Kids stood in long lines, tickets in hand.

Her heart sunk. Payasa had had the tickets. How was she going to get inside now?

She took a deep breath and pushed in front of a guy, then squeezed forward, joining a group of girls dressed in slashed leggings, microminis, and jeans jackets customized with chains.

Jimena laughed with them and acted as if she were part of their group. Zipping past the ticket scan, she eased through the turnstile, her hand cupped as if she held a ticket. Her eyes avoided the security guards.

The girls caught on to what she was doing, but instead of becoming upset, they crowded tighter around her, whooped, and pushed her inside.

"Thanks," Jimena muttered. She had started to hurry away, when someone grabbed her arm. She turned and stared into the face of a security guard.

CHAPTER TWENTY-TWO

A CHILL PASSED THROUGH Jimena. She had a strange feeling that the woman watching her wasn't an ordinary security guard. Her eyes seemed unnaturally clear, and her face radiated an angelic grace.

"You're the goddess who helped me before," Jimena said, spellbound.

"Me?" the woman answered with a wry smile. "A goddess?"

Jimena became impatient. "Please, don't play games with me. I need your help."

The woman placed a comforting hand against Jimena's cheek. "I know. Tell me."

Jimena sighed. "I need to save my friends, and the only way to do that is to change the future back to the one that was always meant to be. I don't know if I can."

"You must. It's your destiny." She smiled at her and then glanced down. "Your moon amulet is gone."

Jimena nodded and rubbed her chest, missing the comfort the charm had always given her.

"Perhaps this one will help you." She held a small cameo in the palm of her hand. The face of a beautiful woman was carved into the stone, but when Jimena looked closer she saw the flowing hair was actually a nest of snakes.

"This is the Medusa stone," the woman explained. "After Medusa's death, the ancients continued to believe in her power, and they carved images of her into their shields and breastplates. Her gaze protected them against enchantment and warded off malicious spirits. Be careful with its magic."

Jimena took the stone and had the eeriest feeling that the snakes were writhing in her hand. She tied it around her neck and felt an unfamiliar power sweep through her.

Then the woman spoke to her in Latin. "*Si sine misercordia oppugnabis, tenebrae fies.*"

"If I attack without compassion, I'll become the darkness," Jimena translated into English to make sure she had understood correctly.

The woman nodded.

Jimena stared at her. "But I thought I wasn't supposed to attack." Was the answer that simple? Had the Daughters become so overwhelmed with fear in the face of the Atrox that they had forgotten everything Maggie had told them about never using the tools of the Atrox? She tried to remember, but she didn't think their hearts had been filled with anger or hatred or a need for revenge. Stark terror is what they had felt.

The woman raised an eyebrow as if she had read Jimena's thoughts. "You're misunderstanding.

You must look with compassion at the other Daughters. If you do, then you'll know which one is the traitor."

Jimena considered this. Then she knew.

CHAPTER TWENTY-THREE

J IMENA HURRIED INSIDE, searching for her friends. The houselights went off, and the speaker stacks exploded with music, like a sonic boom shaking through the cavernous arena. Everyone rushed forward, trying to find their seats. The red-shirted security guards swept their flashlight beams over row numbers.

The singer took the stage, bathed in a blue glow. His voice filled the air with sultry tones.

Shafts of light whisked across the audience in time to the beat and Jimena saw the other Daughters. They looked ready to party and then she understood. They had come prepared for battle.

"We were so worried about you," Vanessa said when Jimena finally joined them. She was vamped-out in a lavender bustier, her arabesque tattoo luminescent. She had extended the design with makeup over her chest and spiked her soft curls with strands of purple.

"We weren't sure what to do, so we came here and hoped you'd show up." Catty hugged her. Her makeup gave her a sassy look. She wore an off-the-shoulder T with iridescent pants. Shocks of hot pink flashed in her hair and down her bare arm in body-paint swirls.

Tianna looked seriously ill and smelled of Vicks. She was dressed in a big hoodie with jeans and a T-shirt, a wad of tissues in her hand and a messenger bag over her shoulder. "I have the flu," she explained. "But I didn't want to miss the show."

"Did you find the Scroll?" Serena asked

Jimena. Gold shadow swept from the inside of her eyelids into her hair line, giving her an other-worldly look. Three small rhinestones were glued at the corner of each eye.

"I didn't find the Scroll," Jimena said over the hard-hitting music. "But I know who has it. Tianna doesn't have the flu. Her symptoms are the effects of the Scroll's curse on her body."

"I can't believe you'd betray us." Vanessa turned to Tianna. "You hate the Atrox more than any of us because of what it did to your family!"

"I'm not betraying anyone!" Tianna broke into a dry hacking cough, then she cleared her throat and pulled the Scroll from her bag. "I found the Scroll in Catty's kitchen when I went by to pick her up for Corrine's party. I knew immediately what it was. I wanted revenge, and I'm finally going to have it."

Catty tried to snatch the Scroll away. "The curse will kill you!"

Tianna shook her head. "I'm going to do what the rest of you have been too afraid to try."

"And that is?" Serena asked.

"I'm going to summon the Atrox and destroy it," Tianna said arrogantly.

"You can't!" Vanessa yelled, and tried to rip the Scroll from Tianna's hand. "We don't have that kind of strength."

"I'll win," Tianna answered, her eyes obstinate, jaw set. "I'll follow the path."

"Only Catty can follow the path." Serena grabbed for the Scroll and missed. "She's the heir."

An eerie tension gathered around them as if something important were about to happen. The room seemed to tremble, and Jimena knew it wasn't from the music this time.

"You've already summoned it, haven't you?" Jimena said.

"You know I have," Tianna answered.

"How could you be such a traitor?" Vanessa asked.

"She isn't," Jimena explained as a disquieting energy continued to build. "She's been tricked into believing that if she summons the Atrox, we'll have the power to destroy it."

A sinister cold swept over them, and the air tingled unnaturally. For the first time doubt hovered in Tianna's eyes. A faint roar resonated through the center like faraway thunder heralding a fierce storm.

Tianna stared at the black shadow easing into the west side of the arena as if hypnotized by what she had summoned.

Jimena lunged forward and grabbed the Scroll from Tianna, then latched onto Catty's arm. "Take us back in time! If we hide the Scroll in the past before Tianna finds it, then maybe the future will change back."

Catty's eyes dilated and the hands on her watch began spinning backward. Blinding light burst around them and they were sucked into the tunnel. They whirled downward at incredible speed, then without warning they fell back into time.

Jimena landed, snapping her chin against the floor, and continued to skid across the linoleum in Catty's kitchen. Catty slammed against the cupboard under the sink.

"You really have to work on these landings." Jimena placed the Scroll on the kitchen table and rubbed her chin. "Let's return to the concert and see if bringing the Scroll back changed anything."

Energy crackled around Catty, but as the force started to draw them into the tunnel, Jimena had a horrible sense of déjà vu. This was exactly the way she had seen the Scroll lying on the kitchen table when she had fled Catty's house Friday night. Distant sirens broke the quiet and then she understood. By bringing the Scroll back, she and Catty had accidentally set everything into motion.

"We've made a mistake!" Jimena strained against the pulling power of the tunnel. "We brought the Scroll into the past for Tianna to find. Remember how you said you didn't understand how it could just appear?"

"Yes," Catty answered, blinking as if she were trying to restrain her power.

"It was us!" Jimena explained. "This has to be the one thing I need to change." But as she reached for the Scroll, the air ruptured, and they were wrenched into the tunnel.

They spiraled down, speeding back to the future.

Catty looked distressed.

"What's wrong?" Jimena asked.

"My landings are always messed up, but not this badly," Catty explained. "I was trying to take us to Maggie's apartment, so how did we end up in my kitchen?"

Jimena shook her head. "I thought that was where you wanted to go."

"No way," Catty continued. "I studied my watch like I always do and thought we had traveled back four days, so how did we end up only two nights back?"

"Maybe you were nervous," Jimena allowed, but secretly she wondered if the sorcerer Chris had warned her about had sent them off course. Could Gerard de Molaire be that powerful?

"Hold on!" Catty shouted.

The tunnel ripped open and they flipped into the air, tumbling to the ground. They landed with a loud thud and lay sprawled on a hard floor. An ear-piercing noise surrounded them, and fires shot into the air.

"Where are we?" Jimena yelled, but she didn't think Catty could hear her over the harsh discordant blare.

▼

CHAPTER TWENTY-FOUR

"I DON'T KNOW WHERE we are!" Catty yelled in panic, scrunching her face.

Then a white light washed over them. A guy in a leather vest, holding a guitar, stepped into the beam next to Jimena. He started to play a fast bone-chilling riff.

"We're on the stage!" Jimena shouted, suddenly aware that the deafening noise came from the yelling spectators.

Drums thundered behind them and more fires rocketed into the air.

The audience shrieked, stomped, and applauded, then broke into song, singing the lyrics louder than the band. Spotlights zigzagged over the kids pressed together, arms pounding over their heads with the beat.

The lead singer walked over to Jimena. His curly hair now wet and clinging to his forehead, neck, and collar. He danced next to her, the hem of his black jeans brushing against her, then gave her a flirtatious grin, offered her his hand and helped her stand.

He sang and slipped his arm around her. Reluctantly, she pulled away and ran to the edge of the stage.

Catty was right behind her. "I bet you'll never complain about my landings again!"

"Right," Jimena answered. "Not until next time."

Security guards were waiting for them behind the footlights, trying to grab their ankles and bring them down. Jimena's heart sunk.

"What are we going to do now?" Catty yelled. "We don't have time to explain things to them."

"Like they'd believe us anyway." Jimena looked frantically around.

One of the guards started to climb on stage.

Suddenly, the fans surged forward, hands waving in the air, screaming, "Dive! Dive!"

The guitar erupted into a barrage of notes as if encouraging them to jump.

Jimena glanced at Catty, then took a deep breath, and made a headlong plunge over the security guards onto the sea of hands. Kids grabbed her legs, waist, arms, neck, and head, and pulled her back to safety away from the guards. Catty floated behind her. Finally, two guys eased them down to the floor.

"That was so cool!" Catty yelled, and then her smile faded into a grimace. "I can still feel the Atrox."

Jimena's body prickled with fear and she glanced west. A shadow continued to creep over the wall. "How did Tianna translate the Scroll?"

she asked. "She doesn't know Latin the way we do."

Catty looked around as if searching for Tianna. "It was even difficult for my mom to translate, and she's a scholar."

"There's no way Tianna could have figured out how to summon the Atrox on her own," Jimena concluded as a new thought came to her. "So who helped her?"

"Let's find out." Catty started shoving through the crowd.

When they finally got back to the others, Vanessa and Serena were somberly watching the ominous shadow, not the concert. Their moon amulets cast out a rainbow of lights.

Tianna looked terrified and ashamed, her lips trembled, and she clutched her amulet in her hand. "I'm sorry."

Jimena tried to put a comforting arm around her, but Tianna recoiled as if she were afraid Jimena was going to hit her.

"Who helped you translate the Scroll?" Jimena asked.

"Professor Hendrix," she answered.

"That's impossible," Serena insisted. "Professor Hendrix knew nothing about the Scroll. I did a mind scan on him."

Tianna shook her head in disagreement. "Saturday, Derek and I took the Scroll over to him. He asked me to leave the Scroll with him, then later that day he gave it back to me along with this translation." She pulled a worn paper from her pocket.

Catty snapped it away and quickly read it. "He tricked you," she said. "This isn't the path."

"I think Professor Hendrix is a sorcerer named Gerard de Molaire," Jimena replied, and told them briefly what Chris had told her. Then she looked at Serena. "You wouldn't have been able to read his thoughts. He's too powerful."

New worry crossed Catty's face. "What about my mom? I mean she's involved with him!"

"Maybe if we can steal the Scroll away from him before he gives it back to Tianna, we can—" But before Jimena could finish speaking, the air began to waver. Catty clasped her hand.

The tunnel split open with an explosion of sparks and they were sucked inside, traveling back in time at breakneck speed. The free fall was uncontrollably fast and made Jimena's stomach ripple. She gasped for air and felt dizzy.

Without warning the tunnel ruptured and they fell, sliding down the hallway that Jimena recognized from their visit to UCLA on Saturday. They smashed into the wall next to the door to Professor Hendrix's office.

Jimena stood abruptly and swayed, then shook her head against the dizziness. "Why did you bring us back so fast?"

"I didn't." Catty jumped up. "I told you before some other force is pulling us along." She started walking away. "I'm going to check on my mom."

Jimena nodded and slipped inside Professor Hendrix's room. A stale tobacco smell mixed with the spicy aroma of cloves and nutmeg hit her. She breathed deeply. It was an unusual scent for an office. She opened a filing cabinet drawer. Bottles filled with herbs, dried flowers, and powders were lined up inside. She wondered if he used these in some secret alchemy.

Footsteps tapped outside the door. She slipped behind a bookcase and peered back into the room from between two stacks of manuscripts.

Professor Hendrix entered the room with Lizelle, Azera, and Zonda, now in their California beach-girl disguises, their hair long and flowing over golden tans.

Another person walked with them. Jimena almost cried out. It was Payasa. They hadn't killed her after all. They had only taken her into the past back to Professor Hendrix. She looked zombied-out, as if some spell had been cast over her.

"You brought the wrong one back from the future." Professor Hendrix grabbed a book from his desk and threw it across the room.

Lizelle ducked and stared obstinately at him, her eyes wide and bewitching. Talons stretched from the tips of her fingers, as if her anger had made them appear. Zonda and Azera hovered behind her.

"You were supposed to bring Jimena to me," he said in frustration. "How many times do I have to tell you where to locate her?" He let out a long breath, his expression austere.

The professor unlocked a desk drawer and pulled out the Scroll and a glass orb. He set the Scroll on the desk and placed the orb on his palm. It caught the light and sent back a kaleidoscope of color. The nymphs hovered around it, staring deep inside the prism.

"I could look in here," he said. "And find Jimena again, but if I send you back in time to make another anonymous call to the police, I have no guarantee you'll be successful." An odd smile crossed his lips. He let the globe float up in the air and then whipped a handkerchief from his pocket and threw it over the glass ball. When he yanked the cloth away, the orb had vanished.

The nymphs jerked back, startled.

He smiled, pleased with himself. "That's why I have summoned Jimena here." He ran a finger over the edge of the Scroll. "Come out, Jimena."

She hesitated, wondering how he could know

she was hiding in the room. Had he seen her? She was certain he couldn't have.

"It was so easy to bring you to me, Jimena." Professor Hendrix sounded pleased with himself. "If only I had known, I would have done that in the beginning. Now show yourself."

"You didn't summon me, Gerard," Jimena argued as she stepped to his desk. "I came on my own." But as she spoke a bolt of fear shot through her. Catty had said some other force had been pulling them forward. Could he be that strong?

He grinned as if reading her thoughts. "So you understand who I am now." Then with a flick of his head, he motioned the nymphs to attack.

Lizelle stepped toward her, her talons reflecting the fluorescent lights. Jimena gazed into her eyes, and her mind drifted into a trance. The dreamy feeling stopped abruptly.

A surprised look covered Lizelle's face. "She wears the Medusa stone."

Zonda and Azera stared at the charm around Jimena's neck, their melodious voices surging with joy as they started to transform. Wings rose from their backs in a luxurious sweep, then flapped in a frenzy, making papers swirl around the room.

Jimena clasped the Medusa stone, hating the slithering feel of the snakes, and watched Zonda, Azera, and Lizelle dissolve into a reddish-gold vapor and disappear. She had an odd feeling that she had freed them.

"The Medusa stone may have saved you from the nymphs, but not from me," Gerard said with sudden rage. "Have you ever fought a sorcerer before?"

He didn't wait for her answer, but lifted his hand. As he did so, it felt as if a sword had cut through her. His eyes narrowed in concentration, and his lips moved with evil's song.

Jimena tried to fight back with her goddess force, but his power was different from any she had battled before. Her mind pulsed with his incantations and her heart thudded slower as pain tightened around her. She bent over, knowing this was the death she had foreseen.

"Payasa!" she yelled.

Gerard laughed. "You wish to say good-bye to your friend. She'll die, too."

Jimena ignored him and yelled again, but this time she clasped the Medusa stone. "Payasa!"

Payasa's head snapped around. She looked stunned. "Jimena?"

Gerard aimed a finger at Payasa.

"No!" Jimena channeled all her energy and seized the Scroll. She handed it to Payasa. "Run!"

Payasa took off, and as soon as she did, Jimena could feel the future opening again.

Gerard lunged after her, his hand pointing at her as if he were going to fire a spell. Jimena brought a foot up and tripped him. He slid into the filing cabinet with a loud crash.

He stared at Jimena, pure hatred in his eyes, then twisted his wrist. The orb appeared in his palm. "I'll find her," he said.

Jimena dove and knocked the glass globe from his hand. It shattered across the floor.

"You've saved the future," Gerard said with a grim twist of his lips. "But at a price. Have you ever heard of a spell that imprisons its victim in endless agony? Did you bargain for that, Jimena?"

"I have won, no matter what the cost," Jimena said defiantly as new pain cut through her.

She began to pray, *"O Mater Luna, Regina nocis, adiuvo me nunc."*

As she continued to whisper the prayer, the woman from her dream appeared and walked toward her, her blue veil shimmering with mystical light.

Jimena knew that all she had to do to escape the spell was to pull the veil from the woman's face and gaze into her eyes. She stretched her arm until her fingers pinched the edge of the silky cloth, then she started to draw it down.

CHAPTER TWENTY-FIVE

CATTY RAN INTO Professor Hendrix's office and dropped to her knees beside Jimena. "Jimena!"

The veiled woman vanished and Jimena stared into Catty's eyes. "He's put a spell on me," she whispered, holding her sides against the pain.

"Not for long." Catty's eyes dilated. Blue sparks crackled around her as she strained to open the tunnel.

Gerard circled his hand and the air spun, winding around them like a gluey cobweb.

"We need some magic of our own," Catty gasped as the gossamer mesh tightened.

Then Jimena remembered what the goddess had told her about Medusa's gaze. She clutched the stone and, with a sharp ripping sound, the tunnel split open behind them. She and Catty were hurled inside. The office roared away in a lightning flash and the last thing Jimena remembered seeing was Gerard's lurid eyes.

"How did you free us?" Catty asked as they plummeted through the darkness.

"Medusa's gaze protects against enchantment," Jimena said, feeling her strength returning.

"Maybe the stone is stronger than Gerard's magic," Catty offered.

"Maybe," Jimena wondered, and then she remembered Catty's mom. "Did you find your mother?"

"No, her assistant said she'd already gone home, so I called her on the phone and told her not to come back to the campus until I had a chance to talk to her."

The tunnel opened, and they fell back into time, landing near the escalator at the Staples Center. No one seemed to notice their sudden appearance. The exits were jammed with kids streaming from the building, anxious to go outside.

"Let's find the others," Jimena said.

"They've found us." Catty pointed and waved.

Vanessa, Serena, and Tianna pushed through the crowd and joined them.

"The Atrox is gone!" Tianna hugged Jimena. "Thank you."

"You stopped Gerard from changing the future," Vanessa added, but then a strange look crossed her face and she glanced at Catty.

Catty looked bewildered. "I think we have a problem."

"What's wrong?" Jimena turned and stared in wonder as someone who looked like her clone walked toward them. "Why didn't my two selves merge?"

"I don't know." Catty looked anxious.

"What happens now?" Serena asked. "Will Jimena always be two people?"

"Her self from the past and her self from the future should have come together in the present," Catty explained.

"But they didn't," Tianna said.

Jimena watched as her replica continued toward her. Then with a gentle nudge the other Jimena pressed into her like a ghost walking through a wall. She felt a tug as her two selves twisted together.

Suddenly, everything felt normal again. She glanced down. Her moon amulet was hanging around her neck, next to the Medusa stone, but she was still wearing the jeans Payasa had given her. She sighed with relief, then touched her hip pocket, remembering her birth certificate and the premonition.

"Let's party now!" Catty yelled.

"I have to go." Jimena started jostling through the throng of kids.

"Where are you going?" Serena grabbed her arm.

"I have to talk to Maggie," Jimena explained. "It's urgent."

"But the slumber party," Serena said, "Stanton will be there and Derek and Michael. It took me forever to get my dad's permission, and Aunt Rita came down from San Francisco to chaperone. You can't back out now."

"I'm not backing out," Jimena explained with rising anxiety. "But I have something I need to do first."

Reluctantly, they walked outside with her down to Figueroa Avenue. A taxi swung to the curb and Jimena started to climb inside, but Gerard stepped in front of her, blocking her way.

He lifted his hand, but before he could cast a spell, Catty, Serena, Tianna, and Vanessa ran up to Jimena, their moon amulets on fire, and pulled her away. Their eyes dilated with the energy growing inside them, and in the odd purple cast of neon lights from the Staples Center their faces looked otherworldly.

Jimena locked arms with them and a luminous aura flickered around their heads.

Gerald stood sideways and stretched his hand. A vortex of light burst from the tips of his fingers and shattered the night.

Before the spiraling energy reached the Daughters, a gold radiance seeped from the Medusa stone and spread around them, forming a shield. As Gerard's volley struck the shimmering barrier, a flurry of tiny flames showered over them.

"Your necklace protected us," Catty whispered.

Gerard stared at the stone. Jimena sensed that he hadn't really wanted to fight, he was only testing her strength to see how she used the amulet.

He vanished as quickly as he had appeared.

The air was still rippling from his departure when Jimena climbed into the cab.

CHAPTER TWENTY-SIX

THE TAXI STOPPED IN front of a small four-story apartment building. Jimena paid the driver and slipped from the backseat.

The sweet fragrance of night jasmine wrapped around her as she pressed a button on the security panel and waited impatiently.

A voice came over the intercom. "Yes?"

"It's Jimena."

A loud buzz sounded and the magnetic lock opened. Jimena hurried inside. She glanced at her reflection as she ran past the mirrors in the entrance. She had never looked less like a goddess in her life. Tangled hair clung flat against her face. Her skin looked shiny, and she had purplish circles under her eyes. Oil stains from laying on the floor in the garage still covered her jeans and shirt.

She charged up the fire stairs, too impatient to wait for the elevator, then continued around a narrow balcony that hung over a courtyard four floors below. She pulled the birth certificate from her pocket and unfolded it.

Before she could knock, the door opened and Maggie stood before her in a long graceful gown, her moon-colored hair curling over her shoulders.

"My dear Jimena." She didn't seem surprised by Jimena's sudden appearance. She looked at her with love and understanding as if she sensed everything that had happened. "You need a cup of tea."

"I need a hell of a lot more than a cup of tea," Jimena mumbled, and walked inside, fanning herself with the birth certificate.

Maggie led her down a long narrow hallway to the living room. She took a match and lit a line of white candles on the mantel, then lit another grouping of five on a small table.

"Sit," she offered.

As Jimena took her place, Maggie wrapped a warm blanket around her shoulders. Then she brought a tray back to the table and joined her.

"You knew I was coming," Jimena said.

"Milk?" Maggie didn't pause for an answer but poured a little into the bottom of a cup.

"Usually we have to wait for the tea to brew," Jimena went on. "You expected me. What gives?"

"This night is different from other nights. Didn't you see the sky? The full moon is overhead with the constellation of the Seven Sisters." Maggie poured tea and handed the cup to Jimena. "I'm very pleased with what you've done. Now do you have something you want to show me?"

Her heartbeat quickened as she handed Maggie the birth certificate. "You know already, don't you?"

Maggie took the paper, but didn't read it.

Instead, she folded it and gave it back. "I knew you would discover the truth about your real age."

"You knew?" Jimena slipped her birth certificate into her shirt pocket.

Maggie nodded. "Your grandmother never meant to keep it from you, but a long time back your mother lied about your age to the welfare office, because if you were less than four years old, she wouldn't have to start a work program. Later, when you were living with your grandmother, she thought it was easier to keep things the way they were."

Jimena shook her head, wishing she had better memories of the time she had spent with her mother.

"But now you only have minutes left," Maggie continued. "What have you decided?"

"It's too late for me to make a decision," Jimena answered. "I had a premonition that I'm going to die. If my vision is right, my death is only seconds away. I can feel the darkness hovering around me."

"There is always darkness before rebirth."

Maggie patted her hand. "You are only sensing the death of your life as a goddess. Your life will continue, but in a different way. Perhaps in an even more powerful manner. Have you made your choice?"

"I'm not going to die?" Jimena asked. She took a deep breath, afraid to believe it.

"Not in the normal sense," Maggie said. "Now tell me quickly. If you fail to make a decision, the outcome can be ghastly. What have you chosen?"

Jimena thought for a moment. "If I hadn't had the premonition of my own death, I wouldn't have been forced to think about life and how much it means to me. Now I know I don't want to leave and become something else. I have too many hopes and dreams for this life. Am I being too selfish?"

"Not at all," Maggie assured her.

"I mean, I always thought I would choose the metamorphosis," Jimena went on. "I figured I'd change into something else, like one hell of a guardian angel, but now . . ." she hesitated.

"What?" Maggie asked.

"I want to stay," she explained. "But I don't want my friends to think I was too afraid to make the transformation."

"Why would they think that?" Maggie asked.

"You always said it was the ones who were afraid to make the change, who stayed."

Maggie looked disappointed. "You only have seconds left to make the most important decision of your life, and you're worrying about other people." She shook her head. "The Atrox gives us foolish worries to distract us from doing what we know is right."

"The Atrox is doing this to me?" Jimena asked.

"Yes." Maggie nodded. "If you know in your heart that what you are doing is best for you, then you can't be concerned with anything else."

"All right, but what about Payasa? What will happen to her?" Jimena asked. "She knows who I am now and when I see her next time I won't be a goddess."

"Payasa won't remember what you have told her, and she'll very happily forget her encounters with the nymphs and Gerard. She'll only remember that you are her friend again."

"And me? Will it be like I have amnesia?" Jimena asked, feeling a pressure building around her.

"You will remember everything, but from a different perspective," Maggie assured her.

"I want to stay," Jimena said with certainty. "More than anything, I want to remain on earth."

"You have made the right choice." Maggie stood.

"You knew?" Jimena asked.

"Of course, I knew, but you had to make the decision on your own." She held out her hand. "Now, come with me so you can experience the mystery of the moon's renewal, the rite of death and rebirth."

▼

CHAPTER TWENTY-SEVEN

J IMENA STOOD ON Serena's porch and ran her fingers through her hair. She didn't quite understand her elation. Maybe it was because she was anxious to see Collin and her friends. She glanced at the moon again, intrigued by its shimmering beauty. Finally she started to knock and the door swung open.

"I thought I caught your thoughts." Serena had changed into sweats.

"You heard me out here?" Jimena walked inside. "Was I that loud?"

Serena looked puzzled. "Where's your moon amulet?"

"Which necklace do you mean?" Jimena replied, as they stepped into the dining room.

"Are you kidding me?" Serena asked, and then her face changed. "You're serious."

Serena's father sat at the massive table. Papers and a laptop computer were spread in front of him.

"Happy birthday, Jimena." Serena's father spoke quietly. Jimena rarely saw him.

"Thank you, Mr. Killingsworth."

Aunt Rita sat at the other end, drinking coffee, and reading a book. "Don't forget to bring me a piece of cake," she warned with a big smile.

Jimena followed Serena through the swinging doors into the kitchen. Streamers and balloons decorated the ceiling, counters, and windows. Vanessa started singing "Happy Birthday," and everyone joined in a loud and rowdy performance.

Tianna slipped a paper cone hat onto

Jimena's head and snapped the elastic band against the bottom of her chin.

When they finished singing, Collin popped a balloon and Derek threw confetti.

Catty grabbed Jimena's hand and led her over to the table. Vanessa and Michael lit the sixteen candles set on a huge chocolate cake.

Stanton stood in a corner, hands in his pockets, a wry smile on his face. Jimena wondered why she had disliked him so much before. He seemed okay now.

"Blow out your candles!" Collin shouted impatiently.

Jimena started to huff and stopped. "You only have sixteen candles." She swiped her finger around the edge of the cake and licked the frosting.

"You're sweet sixteen." Collin nuzzled against her ear.

Jimena pulled the birth certificate from her pocket. "I'm seventeen."

"No way." Vanessa snapped the paper from her, read it, then silently passed it to Catty.

After a moment, Catty looked up, her

playful manner gone, and handed the certificate to Serena.

"I don't need to read it," Serena said softly, staring at Jimena, her eyes wide.

Tianna took it, and as soon as she started reading her expression became somber.

"Why are you all looking at me so strangely?" Jimena asked.

Serena's eyes were glassy with tears now.

"Serena?" Jimena wondered at the odd way they were studying her. "Someone tell me what's wrong."

"Put another candle on the cake before the frosting catches on fire," Serena ordered and wiped her eyes. "Nothing's wrong."

Vanessa shook another candle from the box, then she lit it and stuck it on the cake at an odd angle.

Jimena took a deep breath and blew, extinguishing all seventeen flames at once.

"I hope my wish comes true," she yelled, feeling an overpowering sense of happiness.

Collin whisked her to a corner of the room.

"I love you, Jimena," he whispered. "You stayed with me."

"Where was I going to go?" she asked, perplexed.

He pulled a small velvet box from his pocket and handed it to her. Jimena lifted the lid and stared down at a gold band with a small crescent moon on it.

"It's a promise ring," he whispered.

She shivered with pleasure as he traced one finger over her lips.

He took the ring from the box and slipped it on her finger, then smiling, he cupped his hands around her face. His touch sent a shiver through her. She closed her eyes and he kissed her.

He held her tightly and when he released her, she held up her hand. "Look, everyone!"

Michael smiled and Stanton applauded. The others joined in, but they seemed downhearted.

"I've had enough of these sad looks," Jimena said. "Did you guys forget how to party?"

She walked over to the CD player set up on the counter near the table, found a fast-moving song, and put it in. She turned the volume up until the music pounded through her, then she playfully grabbed Serena's hips.

"Come on." She started dancing next to her. "Let's show them what we got."

Serena had never danced so stiffly, but Jimena wasn't going to let anything bring her down.

Finally, Serena smiled and something inside her seemed to loosen. They started working together, their bodies flowing with the beat as they had always done.

"That's it!" Jimena yelled.

Serena laughed and let her hands reach for the heavens. "I guess I'd rather have you this way than dead."

Jimena shook her head. "Serena, sometimes you're just weird."

Then, without warning, a strange feeling shuddered through her as if there were something important she should be remembering, but the thought vanished as quickly as it had come, leaving her with an odd sense that she had lived many lives before this one.

Don't miss the next

DAUGHTERS OF THE MOON book,

The Talisman

MAGGIE STOOD ON the roof of her apartment building. A sad smile crossed her face, mirroring her mixed emotions. It was time for another to take her place. She needed to tell her successor, but how?

A sudden change in the wind jarred her from her thoughts. Her stomach twisted as fear rose inside her. She traced her fingers through the humming currents, gathering and reading the vibrations. She knew with terrible certainty that the Atrox had somehow escaped her binding. It had managed to take human form again, but how was that possible?

She turned and hurried back to her apartment, praying she wouldn't be too late this time. As she rushed down the stairs, the memories of her early life in ancient Greece came flooding back.

* * *

431 B.C. Penelope stole through the streets of Athens, her pale moon-colored hair flowing behind her. She stopped and peered around the corner into the next alleyway. She had to be careful. Her father would be angry if he discovered she had gone out alone at night again.

She bounded down a long staircase, but as she passed the spring house where the women and slaves gathered each morning to draw water, she became aware of other footsteps and darted inside the small building.

After waiting for the footsteps to pass, she started to leave, but odd, muffled voices made her stop. She pressed back into the darkness and held her breath, listening. Beneath the sound of gurgling water came low eager whispers.

She peered out at the night. In the distance a dim orange glow lit the moon shadows, and before long, a lone soldier came out from a corridor, carrying a torch. He staggered forward drunk, but it was the movement behind him that held Penelope's attention now. Shadows twined and rolled over each other as if regrouping and preparing for some purpose. A slice of shade slipped over the man's shoulder and clung to his cloak. The man seemed foolishly unaware of the dark fog curling around him.

Then a tall man stepped from a nearby stretch of cloudy shadows. The fold of his cloak was pulled over his head, making a hood that hid his face. He grasped the soldier's shoulder, his fingers long and white.

The soldier dropped the torch and thrust his hand back, reaching for the hilt of his sword, but before he could draw the blade, other men appeared from the shadows and crowded around him. His eyes grew wide with terror as a deafening shriek filled the air. The soldier's lips remained parted and a thick white mist wreathed from his mouth. Penelope watched, both fascinated and repulsed, as the men surrounding him nudged hungrily closer, like a pack of starved wolves, breathing in the vapor.

Whatever the man had been now spun into the darkness like a plume of smoke. Then it was gone.

A heavy and unbearable quiet had returned and except for the gurgling of the spring waters and Penelope's own jagged breathing, it was as if the world had stopped. She shuddered, feeling a terrible guilt descend upon her. She should have helped the soldier, but how could she have stopped them? Penelope stepped back and plunged her hands into the cold water behind her, then held them against her cheeks, desperately trying to calm herself.

"Never again," she whispered. . . .

LYNNE EWING is a screenwriter who also counsels troubled teens. In addition to writing all of the books in the Daughters of the Moon series, she is the author of two ALA Quick Picks: *Drive-By* and *Party Girl*. Ms. Ewing lives in Los Angeles, California.